IF I WERE YOUR WOMAN

". . . I'm under the influence."

"No, you're not."

"Yes, I am," Drake said, running his fingers along the curve of her neck and tenderly kissing the softness of her skin. He cupped her face between his hands. "I'm under the influence of you." Then his mouth crushed hers. He could hear his own heartbeat raging in his chest as he ravaged her lips. His tongue explored the recesses in her mouth, discovering softness, sweetness.

He released his lips from her mouth but held her close. "I want to make love to you. I need to make love to you," he whispered. "Can I?"

Desire gripped her as if it had claws. Desire claimed her from the top of her head to the heels of her feet. Desire commandeered the sane part of her brain. Desire was in full control. There was only one way to escape from its grip. Surrender.

Satin could only whisper, "Yes."

IF I WERE YOUR WOMAN

Robin Allen

ARABESQUE

★BET

BOOKS™

BET Publications, LLC
http://www.bet.com
http://www.arabesquebooks.com

ARABESQUE BOOKS are published by

BET Publications, LLC
c/o BET BOOKS
One BET Plaza
1900 W Place NE
Washington, DC 20018-1211

First Printing: October 2002
10 9 8 7 6 5 4 3 2 1

Printed in the United States of America

To my parents
William and Julia Hampton

And my children
Cara and Cassidy Allen

Prologue

"Wilbur . . . Wilbur Frederick Jenkins," the seventy-year-old woman whispered into her twin's ear.

"My dear sister," Maggie said, squeezing her sister's gnarled hand. "You ain't spoken that man's name in over fifty years. Don't go getting yourself all upset now."

"I've thought about him every day. He been in my mind and my heart every day of my life," Maddie said. "I don't speak about him, but he been in my heart."

"I know, honey, I know. I just wish you could have found someone else to love." Maggie peered at the hospital monitors, even though she didn't understand what she was seeing. "Too late for regrets."

Maddie struggled to smile. "I ain't the only one with regrets. Wilbur told me so himself. He told me he married the wrong woman."

"Did he now?" Maggie asked, wondering if the medication Maddie was taking was affecting her memory.

"He did, indeed. Came to visit me a long while back when I was at work."

"At Miss Susan's place?"

"Yeah, he told me that he really didn't love his wife. He thought he loved her, but then he set his eyes on me."

"He done already married and had a family," Maggie said, remembering the devastation that had lasted a lifetime.

"He jilted me. That's what he did. Broke my heart into a million pieces. When you break glass you can't put it back together."

"You keep on living."

"That's what I tried to do. Just keep living. I know everyone thinks I'm the crazy old maid. For a time I hated Wilbur for leaving me. He put a powerful pain in my heart and made me hate all men. I ain't crazy. I just didn't want to be hurt again."

"I know."

"I didn't hate Wilbur for long," Maddie said. "I couldn't."

"Hate isn't good for your soul." Maggie picked up the cup of water and placed the straw in her twin's mouth.

Maddie sipped the water. "You know I ain't changed my will. I know you wants me to, but only you and our nieces in my will."

"That's going to stir up trouble. Lula going to be real upset that her son don't get nothing."

"She shoulda had a girl."

"Maddie, now you—"

"It don't matter none to me. I ain't going to be around when they starts to complain." Maddie cleared her throat. "I have a secret, Maggie. Something I ain't told nobody."

A puzzled expression formed on Maggie's face. "How you keep a secret from me?"

"I just ain't tell you."

"Tell me what?"

"I used to steal time with Wilbur."

"What you mean?"

"He used to come visit me at work. We would just sit in Miss Susan's gazebo and talk. We was stealing time together. Just sit and talk and pretend that time wasn't moving."

Maggie covered her mouth with her hand. "Why didn't you tell me?"

"If I told you, we couldn't do it."

"How long you see him?"

"Maybe ten years. He would just come by. I never knew when he was coming or how long he was staying."

Maggie stared at her sister, surprised that she'd kept a secret for so many years.

"You know the best thing about stealing time?" She met her twin's gaze. "It was our time."

Maggie nodded.

"Wilbur used to say, 'If only I was your man.' And I would say, 'If only I were your woman.'"

A loud piercing sound erupted from the machines attached to Maddie.

Doctors and nurses rushed into the room, but Maggie knew in her heart their efforts would be in vain and they wouldn't be able to save her twin. "Sweet Jesus, Maddie, I love you, dear sister."

"I love you. Time will come when I'll see you again," Maddie squeezed her twin's hand. With her last breath, she muttered, "Wilbur, Wilbur . . ."

One

*Meet Satin Holiday, who is engaged
to a man she doesn't really love*

Satin Holiday wasn't truthful when she told her fiancé that her unexpected trip to Atlanta was job related. Her fiancé had no reason to question her veracity. As a product specialist for a software company, Satin frequently traveled to attend meetings, conferences, and training classes. But the purpose of this trip wasn't related to her current position; its purpose involved interviewing for a different job.

When the woman from an executive search firm called about a higher-paying management position with a high-tech company, Satin's interest was aroused. The position was in Atlanta, Georgia, but she lived in Cleveland, Ohio, and had no desire to leave. Even though she had relatives in Atlanta and spent summer vacations there, relocating was the last thing on her mind.

But the headhunter called several times, and with each conversation, Satin's interest in the position grew. By the time the headhunter called the fourth time, the position sounded like the job of her dreams. So she rearranged her schedule and caught an early-morning flight to Atlanta, Georgia.

Twelve hours later, she didn't know if she felt

guiltier about lying to her fiancé or wanting the job.
The headhunter's description of the position had
been accurate, and it was exactly what Satin wanted.

Satin sailed through the interview with Human Re-
sources. She suspected the woman was new to
recruiting as she asked typical interview questions. The
interview with the hiring manager didn't follow interview protocol. Randall Cunningham, the director of
marketing, described his background in marketing before asking scenario-based questions. Satin delivered
well-thought-out, knowledgeable, polished answers. By
the time he asked a third question—a complicated marketing scenario—Satin decided that she would like to
work for him.

The interview continued over lunch; Randall
shared detailed information about the company's
plans to launch several new products. The more he
talked about the position and the company's culture
of independent thinkers and creative doers, the
deeper her interest.

At times he spoke as if she had the job: "You'll be
working closely with Ed" or "You'll also be responsible
for marketing communications." Randall's final remarks were very positive; he even insinuated that he
wanted to hire her, but the decision would be jointly
made. The interview process was not yet over. An interview with the senior vice president of marketing
was scheduled for the following day.

Satin returned to her hotel. The blast of coolness
from the air-conditioning was a stark reminder of the
differences between Cleveland and Atlanta weather.

In the bathroom, she leaned over the sink and
splashed water on her face. She dried her face and
then applied a light coat of caramel-brown foundation. She applied makeup: blush on her high

cheekbones, eyeliner under almond-shaped eyes, and lipstick on full lips. She brushed her long black hair.

The telephone rang, but she didn't answer. Seconds later her cell phone rang. She didn't answer it, either. She knew who it was—Troy Moss, her fiancé. She didn't want to perpetuate her lie.

Besides, she wasn't in the mood to talk to him. Troy would ask for a detailed account of her activities and then provide an elaborate description of his day. A senior sales executive for an industrial company, Troy was committed to his job and often told her the most mundane things.

Eventually he would ask about their wedding date. Satin avoided the subject as much as possible, but lately it seemed every conversation ended with a discussion about their wedding. She never committed to a specific date, explaining that it would take a year to plan an elegant, elaborate wedding.

However, Troy was becoming impatient, extremely impatient. Six months had passed since his proposal. He was anxious to see wedding plans in action.

Satin didn't share his impatience or enthusiasm. She'd hoped attending a bridal show would give her I'm-getting-married fever, but it had the reverse effect. She felt a claustrophobic sense of doom. At the time, she didn't know why she had such an averse reaction. It wasn't the wedding paraphernalia that unnerved her. It wasn't the prospect of marriage that gave her a sinking feeling in her stomach. It was Troy.

Satin didn't know what to do about it—yet. So she avoided him.

Besides, she had a practical reason for not answering the phone. She had an appointment in fifteen minutes and didn't want to be late.

Her destination—Dailey's Restaurant—was around

the corner from the Westin Peachtree Hotel where she was staying.

Satin arrived early, partly because she was a compulsively prompt person and partly to debunk the myth that black folks are always late. Her penchant for punctuality came from her aunt's influence. Aunt Betty often said, "Punctuality is a reflection of character. And because promptness is so rare, you'll be remembered."

Dailey's was one of her favorite restaurants in Atlanta. The white cloths on the table glowed in the waning light; the glass and silverware gleamed. The starched napkins had been folded into complicated shapes.

"I know I'm late," Zandra Nelson said to Satin when the waiter escorted her to her friend's table.

"And I'm just so surprised," Satin teased, standing up. They warmly hugged. "It's so good to see you." She gave her friend a quick once-over, immediately noticing a change in Zandra's physique. "You've lost weight."

"Yeah, girl." Zandra tugged on the jacket of her pinstriped pantsuit. "Size twelve," she proudly said.

"You look marvelous," Satin said, sitting back down.

"Thank you. You're looking fabulous as usual." Zandra settled into the chair, and removed the napkin, placing it on her lap. "How did the interview go?"

"Excellent! I thought the headhunter exaggerated the job, but she was right on target. It would be a great opportunity for me. A promotion—"

"Oh, yes!"

"More money—"

"A woman needs to get paid."

"Believe it or not, I'd really like to work for the company. The man who would be my boss isn't a micromanager, he's—"

"Hey, hey," Zandra said, tapping on Satin's French-tipped manicured hands. "Where is your ring?

"Oh . . . I'm not wearing it."

"I can see that. Where is it? Did you lose it?"

Satin shook her head. "It's in my purse," she said, reaching for her Coach handbag on the chair, unzipping the inside pocket, and retrieving the diamond ring. She slid the ring on her finger and draped her hand across the table.

"Girl, it's stunning. You got a rock there."

"I know." Satin looked at the ring, wiggling her fingers. "I didn't pick it out, but it's a beautiful ring." She made eye contact with Zandra. "He really surprised me. We talked about getting married one day, but we've been saying that for three years." She glanced at her ring. "Out of the blue, Troy decides that 'one day' is now."

"And you guys are the perfect couple," Zandra said.

Satin's response was interrupted as the waiter arrived to take their orders. After much discussion and contemplation they ordered the same thing: clam chowder and the seafood sampler.

"I hate that," Satin said when the waiter departed from the table.

"Hate what?"

"You're a 'perfect couple' crap."

With a wicked grin on her face, Zandra teased, "You are a perfect couple. The perfect couple. The couple of the year."

A mean glare was Satin's response.

"So what's the deal with the perfect couple?" Zandra asked.

Satin just looked at her, pretending to be unaffected.

"Okay, I'll stop messing with you," Zandra said. The teasing tone turned solemn with sincere concern. "I know something's wrong. I can hear it in your voice. You're not excited about getting married. You didn't call me screaming, 'I'm getting married!' It was like an afterthought. 'Oh by the way, I got engaged.' "

"You know I was never in a hurry to get married."

"Satin, it's not like you're fresh out of college. You and Troy have been together for a while." She sipped some ice water with lemon. "It's time."

"That's what everyone says. It's time." A wrinkled brow reflected her confusion. " 'Time for what?' is my question." Satin paused, then touched her cheek in thought. "Time for a new ending or a new beginning."

"What do you mean?" Genuine surprise appeared on Zandra's face. "If you felt that way, why did you accept the ring?"

Satin released a sharp, hollow laugh. "What woman turns down a two-carat diamond ring?"

"I wouldn't," Zandra agreed.

"He proposed to me at a big party. My family was there. His family was there. How could I say no?"

Zandra nodded, understanding on her face.

"Nobody was surprised. I was probably the only one surprised."

"You didn't know at all?"

"He caught me off guard. Every once in a while he would mention that it's time to get married and we should start thinking about having a family. I told him I want to finish law school, but he's always acted strange whenever I mentioned law school."

"You didn't want to hurt his feelings."

"Not like that. Not in front of everyone. I wanted to scream: 'I'm not ready. I'm not ready.' Instead, I pretended I was excited." Reconnecting her eyes with Zandra, she said, "I've been pretending ever since."

Zandra pursed her lips thoughtfully. "You're serious, aren't you?"

"Yes, I am, but no one believes me." Satin changed her voice to become a distorted blend of friends and family: " 'You and Troy been together since college.' 'You and Troy are the perfect couple.' 'You and Troy will have beautiful babies.'" She ran her fingers through her wavy hair, resentment on her face.

"Is there something you're not telling me? Are you not getting along?"

"That's not it."

"Is he cheating on you?"

"I don't think so."

"Are you cheating on him?"

"Girl, you know me better than that."

Zandra dropped her fork. "Is he abusing you?"

"No!" Satin shook her head with a confused expression on her face. "How did you come to that conclusion? We all went to school together. You know Troy."

"I'm just trying to understand."

"Me, too," Satin said. "I feel like I'm living everyone's expectations of what I should do." Tears suddenly pooled in her eyes. "I'm living a lie and I hate it. I feel trapped because if I don't . . . everyone will be so disappointed."

Struck with the reason for Satin's visit, Zandra asked, "So he doesn't know you're here to interview for another job?"

Satin shook her head.

Zandra lowered her chin and fixed a serious look on Satin. "What do you want? What do you really want?"

Satin's lips parted slightly. A look of frustration crossed her face. She didn't have to pretend. She didn't have to hide the truth that was forcing itself away from her subconscious and forming the words in her mouth that would seem foreign to her family. Hundreds of miles away from her family's perceptions and misconceptions, she was free to release those words.

"Satin, what do you want?" Zandra repeated softly.

She stared across the crowded restaurant before meeting her friend's concerned gaze. "I keep having these bad dreams. I . . . I don't want to marry Troy."

"Are you going to cancel the wedding?"

"I can't."

Zandra squeezed her friend's hand. "It's simple: Don't marry him," she said in a gentle voice.

"It's more complicated than you know."

The mirror revealed a woman dressed for success: navy blue suit, white blouse, navy stockings, and navy pumps. Lightly applied makeup: mascara, blush, and rust-colored lipstick. Simple accessories: small hoop earrings, silver-and-gold ESQ watch, and two rings.

Satin smiled at herself. She was ready for the interview. She grabbed her purse and briefcase and left the hotel.

She dressed appropriately for the interview, but the suit reflected her fashion style: simple, classy, conservative. Self-conscious about her beauty, Satin didn't like to draw attention to her physical appearance, a testament of her mother's often-repeated words: "Inner beauty shines brighter than outer beauty."

As Satin drove into the parking lot of VoiceBox Communications, she remembered her father's advice: "Don't be afraid to show how smart you are." He knew that she had a tendency to downplay her intelligence. *This isn't the time to hide my mind,* she thought. Not while interviewing with the senior vice president. Opening the company's office door, she was struck with a surge of self-confidence. *I'm going to get this job.*

Satin informed the receptionist that she had an appointment with the senior vice president and took a seat. It was an ordinary waiting area: two sofas, two chairs, tables with magazines, abstract paintings. But there was something out of the ordinary in the corner: a grand piano. She was tempted to walk over to the piano and spread her fingers across the keys and play away her anxiety. Soft, mellow music would soothe her nerves.

Instead she picked up a magazine and hoped she wouldn't have to wait long. While thumbing through a trade magazine, the door opened and a tall black man entered. "Tracy . . ." the man said. His deep voice held an edge of delightful surprise.

Satin raised her eyes from the magazine to look into a chocolate-brown face that was intriguingly handsome. He smiled, a half smile of apology. "Pardon me, I thought you were someone else."

Obviously, she was tempted to say, but her mouth was suddenly dry. She politely nodded, a self-conscious smile gracing her face. "No problem."

He smiled again. But it was a different smile. It was a smile that beckoned her. Where, she didn't know.

Satin returned his smile. She couldn't help herself. Who wouldn't smile at a man who had the kind of looks that would make a nun rethink her vocation? Who wouldn't smile at a man with gray eyes? Who wouldn't smile at a man who reeked of an erotic mixture of maleness and cologne?

"Is that your smile or the reflection of mine?" he asked.

Satin stared at him, mesmerized by the glow of his gaze and the intensity of his smile. A moment passed, a moment that allowed for the quiet recognition of souls. "Maybe your smile is a reflection of mine," she finally said.

His brows arched, a hint of humor on his face.

Their smiles deepened as if they'd discovered a unique form of communication. Satin felt as if his smile bathed her, spreading unfamiliar warmth that radiated through her body and soul.

Their flirtatious spell was broken when a woman opened the door and said, "Satin Holiday."

Satin gathered her purse and briefcase and stood. She walked over to the young woman.

"I'll take you to see Mr. Baxter," the perky, young woman said.

"Thank you," Satin said, following her down the hall.

Twenty minutes into the interview, Satin realized she'd spent the night worrying for no reason. Mr. Baxter was a poor interviewer. He didn't inquire about her background, nor did he probe for specifics about her current job. He talked in depth about the company's background, revealing plans for future growth. He frequently digressed to irrelevant tangents that included personal information she didn't need to know.

Maintaining eye contact with the bespectacled gentleman and nodding at appropriate pauses, she was relieved that he wasn't following the typical interview questions. She had forgotten her prepared answers, too busy thinking about the stranger who thought she was Tracy. The way he smiled, the way he dressed, the way he stood, the way he smelled demanded attention.

Hearing Mr. Baxter clear his throat, she realized that he was expecting a response to his question about her current position. But she had been half listening, her thoughts on the man downstairs. "As a senior product specialist, I'm responsible for product positioning, pricing, rollout, and marketing."

"You do understand that even though this position reports to the director of marketing, you will also be working directly with development."

"Yes, I do."

"I have to agree with Randall that you are a good match for this position. We usually don't see eye-to-eye." Mr. Baxter looked at his watch. "I have another appointment, but you'll be hearing from us soon," he said, rising from his chair. "Carol will escort you back downstairs."

"Thank you for your time," Satin said, shaking the man's hand. "I would love the opportunity to join your team."

Striding alongside the secretary, they passed Randall Cunningham's office. Satin saw the man from the lobby sitting with the director of marketing, in the very same chair she'd sat in the day before. The handsome man who smiled at her looked toward the door and they made eye contact—for a fleeting second.

And seemingly seconds later, Satin was in the lobby.

"Before you leave, do you have any questions?" the secretary asked.

"Not at this time." Satin wouldn't dare ask the question that was burning in her mind: *Is the finest man I've ever seen in my life interviewing for the same position?*

Satin unlocked the trunk of her rental car, hoisted her suitcase inside, and slammed the trunk closed. She got inside the car, secured her seat belt, and started the engine. She then removed a sheet of paper from her Day-Timer and placed it on the passenger seat. Directions were on the sheet of paper.

She drove through the hotel's parking lot, exiting onto Peachtree Street and weaving through traffic and turning onto Interstate 75 South. Forty minutes later, she reached her destination: the plot of land she and her cousins had inherited from her great-aunt Maddie Holiday. And somebody wanted to buy the land.

Viewing the vastness and wildness of the land, she couldn't understand why.

Why didn't matter to her cousins. When they all received legal documents from Aunt Maddie's estate offering them $10,000 each to sell the land, everyone was eager to sell except Satin.

But then there was a second offer for $15,000. Satin still wasn't interested, which created a problem for her cousins and the potential buyer. In order for the land to be sold, all the heirs must agree to sell the land.

Satin received another offer for $20,000. Her cousins begged her to sign the paperwork. Getting out of the car, she walked around the property, hoping to discover why the land was in demand.

Satin didn't notice the curtains part in the window on the house across the street. The house sat far back on the road, unseen by the casual passerby.

The occupant of the house, however, noticed Satin. The old man watched Satin get out of the car and walk around the spacious land.

He would have been curious about Satin, even if he hadn't been paid to watch the property. He might not have had a woman in years, but the toothless old coot knew a beautiful woman when he saw one. In his younger days, she would have been forbidden fruit; crossing the color line was taboo, done in secret or against the woman's wishes.

When she turned and began walking back to her car, the old man wondered if she had seen him. He instinctively jumped away from the window, but realized the foolishness of his actions. A thicket of trees hid the house. He peeked out the window again and wrote down the car's license number. He fumbled through a crowded drawer, searching for the developer's business card. The developer offered him money to watch the land, and also assured him that his own land would not be included in the plans for a shopping center and business office park.

The old man looked out the window again, using his binoculars for a sharper view. She was driving away, but he noticed something he hadn't seen before: the car was a rental. He speculated on the possibility that out-of-town developers might be interested in the land. He put on his glasses to make sure he had the right card. The name Richard Creighton was printed in bold letters. The old man picked up the phone and dialed Richard Creighton's number.

TWO

Life puts you to the test when
Mama doesn't know best

"Did you know that Peter tendered his resignation?"

"He did?" Satin gasped, looking wide-eyed at Neal Davis, vice president of product marketing and development. Even though she'd been out of the office for two days, she had checked her E-mail. There weren't any messages about her boss's departure.

She'd seen him earlier, and they merely exchanged cursory greetings. He'd requested a meeting with her for later that afternoon, but gave no indication as to the purpose of the meeting. She presumed the meeting was to discuss the software bugs quality and assurance had discovered. Satin recommended the product release date be delayed until the problem was resolved. Marketing did not agree with her recommendation. She copied her boss and director as to the reasons for her conclusion. So when the director requested an impromptu meeting, Satin presumed that he was going to ask her to support marketing's efforts to meet the release date.

"You look as surprised as I was," Neal said, leaning back in the high-back leather chair. He reached for his cup of coffee. "It seems this company is filled with surprises."

"It's so unexpected."

Neal sipped his coffee, then smiled at her. "I have an even bigger surprise."

"We're merging with IntelliQ," Satin speculated, referring to the recurring rumors about the company's competitor. It was a rumor that floated around for a year.

"Not yet. And if it happens, I don't think many would be surprised."

"Probably not."

"Will you be surprised if I offer you Peter's position?"

Satin's stomach dropped. *Surprised* isn't the word. How about *flabbergasted, stunned—*"

"When you're finished being flabbergasted and stunned, let me tell you I'm serious. Peter and I have discussed the position and we both agree that you're the best person for the position."

For a moment, Satin wondered if they knew she'd interviewed for another position with a different company. Maybe they were setting her up so that she'd turn down the position in Atlanta, take the promotion, and then later Neal would fire her. But Neal had a reputation for being a straight shooter. He didn't play games like that.

Still shocked, Satin scrutinized Neal's face. His expression was intense and serious. A hint of amusement danced in his eyes; maybe he was bemused by her shocked reaction.

"Are you serious?"

"Yes, I am."

"You're offering me Peter's position as . . . product manager."

"I don't know the exact title." Neal fiddled with some paperwork on his desk. "Satin, I've obviously caught you off guard. Do you need time to think about it?"

A moment of silence passed. Satin thought about the position she'd interviewed for in Atlanta. Two weeks had passed and the company hadn't contacted her. And now, uncannily, she was being offered a promotional opportunity similar to the position in Atlanta. An old adage gave her the answer: "One bird in hand beats two in the bush."

Clearing her throat, she looked into Neal's perplexed face. "No, I don't need more time." Excitement about the position grew on her face. She glowed with the prospect of succeeding in the new role. "It will be a challenging role and a great opportunity for growth." She smiled and added, "I like challenges."

"I know you'll do well," Neal said, a half smile on his lips.

Satin unlocked the door to her parents' house. The smell of Pine-Sol, Clorox, and furniture polish assailed her nose as she entered the foyer. It wasn't an unfamiliar smell, especially on Thursdays when her mother devoted the day to cleaning the house from the basement to the attic. The smell triggered childhood memories of Saturdays: clean-the-house day. Satin and her two brothers would have to spend the day mopping the floors, vacuuming the carpets, scrubbing the baseboards, washing and folding clothes, and polishing the furniture.

"Mama," she called from the bottom of the stairs.

"I'm up here," she heard her mother say.

Satin hung her wool coat in the hall closet before going upstairs. She found her mother folding laundry and watching television. *Tomorrow's Light* was her mother's favorite soap opera

"Hi, Mama," she said upon entering her mother's crowded bedroom. Heavy pieces of mahogany furniture filled the room: a four-poster queen-size bed, two nightstands, lingerie chest, and wide dresser. The only pieces of furniture that didn't match the bedroom set were the entertainment center and lounge chair. Satin kissed her mother on the cheek.

"What are you doing here in the middle of the day?" Julia asked, a worried expression on her pecan-brown face.

"I don't know," Satin said, shrugging. "I took a late lunch and didn't feel like going back to work."

Her brows drawn together, Julia asked, "You're not going to get fired, are you?"

"No, Mama." Satin sat on the bed. "Actually, I'm going to be working from home."

"I can't believe companies let you do that. In my day, the bosses had to watch over to make sure you were doing what you were supposed to be doing."

"Some bosses are still like that. It's not something I do all the time. I'll probably be up late tonight working."

"You put in an awful lot of hours, honey." She folded a large thick towel in half and then folded it again. "That's going to have to change when you and Troy get married."

Satin heard that sound again. The sound of a door slamming shut and a key turning, locking the door. It was a sound from a recurring dream, a dream that sometimes turned into a nightmare. The dream began in a church. It was her wedding day, a seemingly joyful day. The wedding ceremony was beautiful. All her family and friends were there; everyone was smiling and having a good time. Then the dream would take an unexpected twist. Suddenly she'd be in jail in her wedding gown. But everyone was still smiling, waving good-bye and blowing kisses. And she'd wake up, feeling frightened and mystified.

Satin didn't respond to her mother's remark. Sometimes she listened to her mother, and sometimes she did not. The challenge was learning when to listen to Mama and when to listen to her heart. Watched the soap opera, Satin asked, "What happened to Caprice?"

"She got arrested."

"That's what she gets for thinking she can get away with anything."

"Jenny and Jason got engaged," Julia said, updating Satin on the soap opera's story lines. "But that was no surprise."

"Not at all."

"I picked up some bridal magazines for you," Julia said during a commercial break. "They have the most beautiful wedding gowns! I saw some you might like. I know we have different tastes, but there's gowns you'll like." Julia pointed to the entertainment center. "Look over there on the middle shelf."

Satin retrieved three bridal magazines from the entertainment center and carried them over to the bed. She opened one and flipped through the pages.

Julia came around to the other side of the bed. "You'll have to wear your hair out." She fingered the strands of Satin's thick hair, bound together into a long ponytail. She kissed her daughter on the forehead. "You're going to be such a beautiful bride." Her voice was filled with maternal pride, her face animated with joy.

Satin gave her mother a half smile. She wondered what her mother would say if she revealed her innermost feelings: *I don't think I love Troy enough to marry him.*

"Have you decided on a date yet?" Julia asked, returning to the other side of the bed.

"No."

"What are you waiting on?"

"I don't know." She released a deep sigh. "Mama, how in love were you with Daddy when you got married?"

"What kind of question is that? I was in love with him. He was in love with me. I wasn't interested in anyone else." She stopped folding towels and gave her daughter a serious look. "Are you interested in someone else?"

Satin shook her head, even though the image of the smiling man formed in her head. She didn't know his name, but for some strange reason, she frequently thought about him. She wondered what kind of life he had: Was he married? Did he have children? Was he happy? A figment of a nameless man definitely would not be considered interest in someone else, she concluded.

"If you're not interested in someone else, don't go pondering the quantity of love. It's immeasurable. And love is ever changing. But it's special and something to treasure. Once you have it, don't squander it with too much thought. I know how analytical you can be, Satin."

"Okay," Satin said, concluding that her mother would never understand her feelings.

"Have you found a place for the reception?"

"Not yet."

"What are you waiting on, honey?" Julia asked, impatience in her voice. "Time is passing by."

"I've just been so busy at work."

"I can help, you know."

"I know, Mama. You told me before."

"Or you can hire a wedding coordinator," Julia suggested. "Somebody that takes care of everything."

Satin nodded. "I've been thinking about hiring one."

"I'm ready to get into action," Julia said. "Your

daddy and I didn't have a big wedding. We just went to the justice of peace." She dropped her voice to a whisper. "I was carrying O.B.," she said, referring to her oldest son.

"We know," Satin said, laughing. "We figured it out a long time ago."

"I wanted a proper church wedding. We couldn't afford anything big or fancy, but something in the church would have been nice," Julia explained, regret in her voice. "Back then, I couldn't get married in the church because I was in the family way. Nowadays they marry you anyway."

"Why don't you and Daddy renew your wedding vows?" Satin posed. "You always talk about wishing you got married in a church. Your thirty-fifth anniversary is coming up."

"It seems so . . . crass."

"People do it, Mama," Satin said.

"Madeleine and Phillipe renewed their vows."

"I'm not talking about characters on a soap opera," Satin exclaimed. "Remember when Mr. and Mrs. Henderson renewed their vows?"

Julia nodded. "It was a beautiful ceremony."

"You kept saying they were going to look silly, but they didn't."

"You know your daddy ain't going to go for it."

"I think he will. I know he will. Especially if he knows it's something you really want to do." She gave her mother an encouraging smile. "Talk to him about it."

"Maybe," Julia said, folding the last towel and placing it on top of the pile of folded towels. "We'll see."

They watched a segment of *Tomorrow's Light* in silence. During the commercial break, Satin said, "I have some good news. My boss is quitting and . . . I've been offered his job."

When her mother didn't respond, Satin explained, "Mama, it's a promotion! More responsibility and more money. I don't how much money—we didn't talk about it," she said, excitement ringing in her voice. "But it's a promotion."

Julia stared at her daughter a moment before asking, "Are you going to take it?"

Satin's mouth dropped open. "What do you mean?"

"Are you going to take it?"

Satin's reaction was defensive. "Why wouldn't I?"

"Because you're getting married."

"What does that have to do with it?" Satin asked, anger creeping in her voice.

"Now that you're getting married, I thought you would start focusing on marriage and not your career."

"We're not married yet," she retorted.

"And you don't want to cause problems in your marriage before you get married."

Julia saw the dark expression on Satin's face, but continued. "You have to let the man be the man. If you keep getting promotions, how is Troy going to feel? How is he going to be the man if you have a better position? That's what's wrong with marriages today. The man is supposed to be the man. And the woman is supposed to be the woman."

"You should be happy for me, Mama," Satin said, standing. "You should be proud of me."

"I am very proud of you. You are a very intelligent, beautiful woman. But I'm just trying to tell how things are supposed to work in a marriage."

Satin heard that sound again, the sound from her dreams: the door slamming shut, the key locking the door.

"Let the man be the man and—"

"Mama, I'm going home now. I have work to do."

"Don't be mad, honey," Julia said.

Satin took a deep breath, then exhaled. "I'm not," she said, realizing the futility of explaining her feelings.

"You still planning to have kids? I want a grandbaby to take care of."

"One day." She shrugged. "When the time is right."

"Good. I know Troy wants children. He's like your father. He wants to be the provider. He'll be a good provider."

Satin walked around the other side of the bed and kissed her mother. "I'll see you later."

"Be careful driving home," Julia said, following Satin into the hall. They reached the stairs. "I don't think you should take the job."

Satin gave her mother a thoughtful glance. "I already have," she said, and went down the stairs.

Troy Moss's name scrolled across the caller ID box. Satin read the name but didn't reach for the phone. The phone rang again, but Satin remained in her chair reading the evening newspaper, *The Plain Dealer*. It rang again; she only had a few seconds to answer before it rolled over to electronic voice mail. This was his third time calling. If she didn't answer, he would soon be knocking at the door. She definitely didn't want to see him.

"Hello," Satin said.

"Satin, are you all right?"

"I'm fine. Just tired." She yawned. "I fell asleep on the couch."

"You're not sick, are you?"

"No, I'm fine."

"I miss you. I want to come over."

"It's late, Troy, and I'm really tired."

"I haven't seen you in almost two weeks. You were gone and then I left for the sales conference."

"How did it go?"

"It went great. I learned a lot about the new incentive program we're going to offer."

"That's good," Satin said.

"I spent a lot of time with my new manager. We really got to know each other. I think we're going to work well together. I have a feeling I'm going to get promoted. It won't happen until the end of next quarter, but I'm certain he's going to recommend me."

"That's excellent. I'm proud of you. You deserve it. I have some good news, too." Satin paused, reflecting on her conversation with her mother. Their views about marriage were so different, they were parallel worlds apart. "I got a promotion."

There was silence on the other end of the phone line. Satin wondered if she stepped into the nebulous world of role definition. Was it a land mine she should have stepped over? "Did you hear me? I got a promotion."

"What kind of promotion?" Troy asked, excitement missing from his voice.

"Peter's leaving and I'll be taking his place."

"Really! What's your title going to be?"

"All the details haven't been worked out. Peter was senior product manager. They'll probably make me an associate product manager."

"What about salary? How much money are we talking?"

"I'm guessing $5,000 or $6,000 more."

"So . . . I'll still be making more money than you." Troy matter of factly stated, his voice heavy with innuendo.

"Why does that mean so much to you?" she asked

indignantly, remembering her mother's remarks, which flashed through her mind like a neon light, blaring danger . . . danger.

"I'm supposed to be the breadwinner in the family. I want to be able to take care of you and our kids when we have them. This position will definitely put me in the six figure range, so even if you want to quit, I can take care of things."

"I never said I was quitting my job!" she said angrily.

"I'm not talking now. I'm talking later. A few years from now."

"I'm serious about my career." She released a frustrated sigh. "I hope you understand that."

"I know you are. And I'm serious about wanting to take care of you."

"I appreciate that. My career isn't—"

"You can have your career as long as it doesn't interfere with us. My daddy used to say there can only be one king of the castle."

"What the hell does that mean?"

"I'm the king and you're the queen. I'm going to take care of you."

"I'm not sure if I like that," she softly said, trying to ignore the deepening sense of fear. It wasn't fear for her life, but fear for her emotional well-being. Fear of a lifetime of compromises in which she'd be swallowed into his old-fashioned view of male and female roles. And she'd slowly suffocate.

"What woman wouldn't want to be treated like a queen?"

"Did you ever hear about the job you interviewed for in Atlanta?" Tyrece Pittman asked Satin as they walked toward the ladies' dressing room after a rigorous aerobics class.

"Not a thing. It's been a month since I went down there." Satin stopped at the water fountain, pressed the water release button, and drank some water. "I guess I didn't get the job."

"At least you got your promotion," Tyrece said before sipping from the water fountain.

"Maybe I'm not supposed to leave. I wasn't looking, anyway. The headhunter was just so insistent that I had to check it out." She blotted the sweat from her face with a towel. "I guess it wasn't meant to be."

"Maybe not." Tyrece opened the door to the ladies' dressing room and Satin followed her inside.

"I wonder if this brother I saw got the job."

"Who are you talking about?"

"While I was in the lobby waiting to be interviewed, this fine—finer than fine—brother came in. He thought I was someone else and said, 'Tracy.' That's when I looked up and stared into the most beautiful gray eyes. He was tall, chocolate, and fine."

"Ooo la la."

"Yeah, girl. He said something about my smile . . . 'Is that your smile or the reflection of mine?'"

Tyrece opened her locker door. "He said that?"

"Those were his exact words."

"And you remember them?"

"Can't seem to forget them. I said, 'Maybe your smile is a reflection of mine.'"

"Go head, girl." Tyrece put sweatpants and a shirt over her leotard and tights.

"My best comeback line ever," she said, laughing. "We were in a place of business so we really couldn't talk. But for some reason I keep thinking about him. I don't even know his name." She sat on the bench and unlaced her aerobic shoes. "I wonder if he got the job."

"The job you interviewed for?"

"After I interviewed with the senior vice president, his secretary was escorting me to the door. We passed the marketing director's office. He had interviewed me the day before. When I passed his office, the fine brother, the smile brother that I had just seen in the lobby, was in there with him."

"So you think he was interviewing for the position?"

"I think so. Just as I passed the office he looked up."

"Who? 'The fine brother'?" Tyrece laughed. "'The smile brother'?"

"Yes. We made eye contact, but it was just for a second. I was thinking, 'He's interviewing for my job.'" She shrugged. "He probably got the job."

"Maybe he did, but then again, maybe he didn't. You don't know."

"You're right," Satin said. "The only thing I know is they haven't called to offer me the job." She slid into a pair of jeans. "Oh, well."

"Girl, I still can't believe you even went on that interview. You're about to get married. I know you didn't tell Troy."

Satin shook her head. "He wasn't exactly thrilled about my promotion."

Tyrece frowned. "Why do you say that?"

"Troy couldn't handle it if I made more money than him. Sometimes I can't believe he has such *Leave It To Beaver* views about marriage." She pulled her sweatshirt over her head. "Sometimes I don't think we should get married."

"Girl, you're just tripping. Everyone would be so shocked and disappointed if you and Troy didn't get married," Tyrece said.

"We're so different in many ways."

"It's hard to find a place of compromise. I know." Tyrece closed the locker door. "I live with it every day."

"So how are things going with you and Bobby?"

"Nothing's changed. It hasn't improved and it hasn't worsened. Kayla is the only reason we're together. She is why we got married in the first place."

"How is little Miss Thing?" Satin said, inquiring about her five-year-old goddaughter.

"Being Miss Thing all day. Trying my nerves." Tyrece closed her locker door. "You know, when you were talking about the brother you met—the smile man—you had that look on your face. That look of excitement."

"I did?"

"Oh, yeah. That undercurrent of . . . passion. That's what's missing in my relationship with Bobby. Somewhere along the way we lost it."

"I don't remember having that kind of feeling with Troy . . . or with anybody. We just fell into a relationship," Satin explained. "We were friends, then we dated, and then we were a couple. Somehow we're everybody's idea of a perfect couple."

"That's because you have similar backgrounds, went to college together, your families know each other, and—"

"I don't care about all that. I want to know what it feels like to have that emotional rush, that love high."

"Come back from never-never land," Tyrece said, waving her hand in Satin's face. "It doesn't last. At least you have things in common so that when that love high comes down, you still have something to work with."

"You're not giving me a lot to look forward to. What if that's not enough? Troy is stable. But a part of me wants to fly. I want to be free . . . to be me."

"Come back to earth, Satin. Back to reality where us little mortals live."

"The reality is I didn't get that job in Atlanta and

the mysterious handsome brother is probably sitting in my office."

"Working your job," said Tyrece.

"Soaring in my skies," said Satin.

"That's stretching it."

"Okay," Satin said. "The smile man got my gig."

"Wait a minute, let's be realistic. If you had gotten that job, would you really leave?"

Satin thought for a moment. "I think so."

"Now you're really tripping!" Tyrece placed an arm around Satin's shoulders. "I can't see you leaving your family and friends. Not all by yourself."

"There's a part of me that really wants to. As long as I'm here I'll be Troy's woman, Julia's daughter, Oliver's baby girl, Justin and O.B.'s little sister."

Three

*Thus we meet Drake Swanson, who
believes women are like his mother*

Drake Swanson picked up the telephone and dialed
411. The automated response system requested he
identify a listing. "Operator, please," Drake repeated
several times until a live operator answered.

"How can I help you?"

"Do you have a listing for Satin Holiday?" Drake
asked.

"What city?"

"Atlanta . . . I guess."

"Do you have an address?" the operator asked.

"No."

"No listing for Satin Holiday," the operator said.

"Okay." Disappointed, Drake was consoled by the
fact that he wasn't requesting the information in person. If his family knew he was trying to track down a
woman he hadn't met, they'd be shocked. Younger
brother Derek would unmercifully tease him and
older brother Damon would endlessly laugh.

"There are several listings for S. Holiday," the operator continued.

"Oh!" Hope rebounded in his voice. "How many?"

"Over thirty. Do you have a street name?"

"No, I don't. Thank you." Drake hung up the telephone. He was just as surprised by his actions, as his brothers would be. Calling 411 to get an unknown woman's phone number was completely out of character. *Here's the 411,* he thought. *You're never going to see her again.*

"Excuse me," a voice said, interrupting his self-deprecating thoughts. "Are you ready to meet with us?"

Drake looked at Brent Norwood, creative director, standing in the doorway, holding a stack of creative comps. "Sure," Drake said, glancing at the clock on his desk. The Art Deco-style clock read 3:00 P.M. "Come on in." Drake rose from his chair and walked over to the large glass-topped conference table.

"Hi, Shana," Drake said to the copywriter. "I didn't see you back there."

"I was hiding," she joked, walking in behind Brent. They both took a seat at the conference table.

"Where's Eric?" Drake asked, inquiring about the graphic designer.

"He's slammed with deadlines," Shana answered. "And they have that presentation to McDonald's tomorrow."

"We have to win that account," Drake said adamantly. "That will put us in position to go after other food service clients. But that's not the purpose of this meeting. We're here to talk about VoiceBox."

"We have some excellent ideas," Brent said. "The fact that they're receptive to nontraditional marketing approaches opens the door to so many possibilities."

"Especially since their technology is incredibly cool," said Shana.

"But they're not the first to come to the market with voice command technology," Drake said. "That's why their advertising and marketing campaign has to be creative, memorable, and—"

"Wicked," Brent said.

"Wicked," Drake said, chuckling. "How many times a day do you say that word?"

"Sit near him and you'll hear it fifty times a day," Shana said. "I counted."

Brent rolled his eyes at Shana. "At least I don't curse all the time."

"All right, fuss with each other later." Drake leaned back in his chair. "Show me wicked."

Brent spread several comp cards across the table, representing five different treatments. He explained the creative direction and marketing messages intertwined within each campaign, including how the ideas were conceived. Shana interjected comments about the copy, pointing out the driving theme for each campaign.

"I told you they were wicked ideas," Brent said.

"Wicked," Shana said, playfully tapping Brent's shoulder, "and incredibly cool."

Drake examined the creative designs for several minutes. "Let's narrow it down to these three," he said pointing to his selection. "This one, 'Always There,' needs something. Maybe better photographs or a different color scheme." He thoughtfully paused. "And this one," he chuckled, "'Ring, Ring, Ring' should be more whimsical, almost like a Dr. Seuss book. Actually, I think that's the one they'll like."

"I wanted to present an option that was similar to their collateral," Shana said, pointing to the "Always There" design.

"'Ring, Ring, Ring' is the best one. I like the feel of it, but something's missing," Drake said.

"Pay up—now," Shana said to Brent, her hand extended across table, palm side up. Drake flashed a curious look at them.

"We bet which one you would pick," Shana said. "I told him you would like 'Ring, Ring, Ring' the best, but he said you would like 'Always There.'"

"I don't know why I bet against you," Brent complained. "I always lose." He placed a five-dollar bill in Shana's outstretched hand.

"I'm always there," she said with a devilish grin.

"Well, look who's finally here," Glenda Swanson said when Drake entered his brother Damon's living room. "I thought we were going to have to drag you out of that office of yours."

"It's Sunday, Glenda," Drake said, hugging his mother. "I only work on Sunday when it's necessary."

"Son, I want you to meet a friend of mine," Glenda said, indicating the gentlemen sitting next to her on the sofa. "This is Henry Jones. Henry, this is my son Drake. He's the one I told you about that runs an advertising agency. He has a partner, but Drake runs the show."

Drake extended his hand to Henry, who was much shorter than his mother. "It's a pleasure to meet you, sir."

"I know Henry from a long time ago," Glenda explained. "He met you before, when you were little."

"Y'all was little fellows," Henry said. "I remember you didn't call her Mama."

"She never wanted us to call her Mama," said Damon, coming into the room with two glasses filled with whiskey and ice. He handed the glasses to his mother and Henry. "Hey," he said to Drake, "want one?"

"No, thanks."

"I was too young for that," Glenda said. "I didn't want people to think I was old. Ain't nothing old about me."

"You got that right, sugar," Henry said, rubbing his hand up and down Glenda's thigh.

Alanna Swanson appeared at the living room doorway. A petite, attractive woman, she could get away with using her college identification ten years later. "Good afternoon, everyone," she said. "I lay down after church. I was only going to take a short nap, but I'm just now getting up."

"Hey, Alanna." Drake lifted his hand in greeting. "Long time no see."

"When you've been here, I was out shopping or running with the kids."

"You feeling all right?" Glenda said, walking across the room. "You don't look so good," she said, and planted an affectionate kiss on her daughter-in-law's cheek.

"I don't feel well," Alanna said, running her brown hands through her mass of braids. "I've been feeling extremely tired. I hate feeling this way. I have to help D.J. with his school project and Lane needs to practice piano."

"I'll take care of the kids." Damon engulfed his wife's petite figure in his football-player frame. "Go back to bed and get some more rest."

"I made the sides for dinner last night," Alanna said. "All you need to do is cook the meat."

"Baby, don't worry." Damon kissed Alanna on the forehead. "Get some rest. I'll check on you later."

"Ain't you something. Still nice to each other after all these years," remarked Glenda. "You the only one in this family that can maintain a relationship."

"That's my baby! Wouldn't know what to do without her," Damon said, chuckling. "Till death do us part."

"You must have gotten that from your father, because you sure didn't get that from me. I'm as restless as tumbleweed. Derek is the same way. Don't know what he wants to do with himself." Glenda paused to sip her drink. "And you, Drake, you got your head on straight about business, but you a little lost when it comes to women. Your problem is you still pining for Tavia."

"Glenda, I am not pining for her," Drake said in a defensive tone of voice. "I'm just not interested in getting involved with anyone."

"That's because you ain't got over Tavia." She returned to the sofa. "Henry, let me tell you what happened. Drake was about to get married. He was standing in front of the church and we were waiting for Tavia to come down the aisle, but she never showed up. She ran off to Hollywood." Glenda rattled the ice in her glass. "Drake took it real hard. He didn't break down and cry. He got too much pride for that. It wounded his pride."

"That's enough, Glenda. You're talking too much," Drake said.

"Damon, can you fix me another one?" Glenda asked, handing him her empty glass.

"Sure," Damon said before leaving the room.

"And you drink too much," Drake added

"I ain't saying you been a monk. You wine and dine women, but you don't let any of them get close to you. You keep them far, far away from your heart." She laughed. "I got your number there. That's the safe thing to do."

"Glenda!" Drake's nostrils flared in irritation.

"I ain't told Henry the whole story. You see, the woman he was going to marry is Tavia Beaudeaux."

"The movie star!" Henry exclaimed. "Mmm, mmm, mmm, she's a fine young thing."

"She's a big-time movie star now. Right up there with Halle Berry and Angela Bassett."

"Just drop the subject!" Drake demanded, although he knew his request would be ignored. Once Glenda had a few drinks in her she became as effervescent as Alka-Seltzer.

"The girl had to what she had to do," Glenda said. "She knew she wouldn't be a star if she stayed in Atlanta."

"I wouldn't have stood in her way," Drake said.

"I'm not mad at her for following her dream. She should have told you before the invitations were mailed." Glenda's tone became indignant. "She was wronger than wrong to wait until the day of the wedding."

"She didn't change her mind until she got that phone call to audition."

Henry's eyes darted between Glenda and Drake. In the moment of silence, he ventured into the conversation. "She's a good actress."

"A damn good actress!" Glenda said. "That's why she followed her dreams."

"Like you did, Glenda," Drake angrily said. "Leaving three little boys to fend for themselves so you could do whatever the hell you wanted to do! Roaming the country and—"

Her eyes narrowed, she defensively said, "I left you with your father. He took good care of you boys."

"All right now," Damon said, returning to the room. "We're not here for that. We've been through this before." He handed the whiskey-filled glass to his mother.

"Oh, yes, we have!" Glenda exclaimed, and then downed some of her drink. "Too many damn times."

"Everyone, chill," Damon said. "Come in the kitchen and help me with dinner, Drake. Better yet, you can help D.J. with his school project."

Several hours later, Drake was the remaining guest at his brother's house. Dinner had been eaten,

Glenda and Henry departed after dessert, and the children were in bed. When Alanna came down to clean up the kitchen, both Drake and Damon sent her back to bed, promising to restore the kitchen to normalcy.

"I hate waking up to a dirty kitchen," Alanna complained, removing plates from the kitchen table.

"I know, baby," Damon said. "We'll handle it."

"We! I've been working all afternoon," Drake jokingly complained. "Cooking the meat, then helping D.J. with math problems I don't ever remember having, and—"

"Thank you, brother-in-law," Alanna said, leaning her head on his shoulders. "You always pitch in."

"That's what families are for," Drake said. "Seriously, Alanna, I'll help Damon and then I'll be on my way. So don't worry about it."

Damon put his arm around Alanna's waist. "I'll be up soon." He whispered in Alanna's ear, "If you're not sleep, maybe we can . . ."

She gave him a tender smile before leaving the room.

"You can't whisper," Drake said. "I heard you."

Damon punched his brother's arm. "Hey, you know how we do. I'll get the table and put everything away. You do the pots and pans."

"Just the way we did it when we were kids." Drake reached under the kitchen sink for the dishwashing detergent. "I don't even know why I'm going to tell you this because I know you're going to laugh."

"But you must got to get it off your chest, huh?" he said, a mirthful lilt in his voice.

Drake shrugged. "I met this woman a few weeks ago. She's beautiful."

"Nothing unusual so far."

"We didn't formally meet. I had an appointment with VoiceBox. I went into their lobby and that's when I see this beautiful woman. I thought she was Tracy

Golden. She does a lot of video work for some of my music clients. I called her name, but it wasn't her."

"Mmm-hmm."

"She looks up at me and she's fine! She looked like a Fashion Fair model waiting to be discovered."

"That fine?"

Drake nodded. "I smiled at her and she smiled back. Then I said, 'Is that your smile or the reflection of mine?'"

"That's definitely not your average pick-up line."

"I wasn't trying to pick her up. We weren't in a club or anything. Before I could introduce myself, someone came out for her."

"So you don't even know her name."

"The receptionist spoke her name when she opened the door. Her name is Satin Holiday. She followed the lady to wherever she was going. While I was talking to the marketing director, she passed by his office. But that was it. I didn't get to talk to her. All I know is her name."

Damon rinsed some plates off before putting them in the dishwasher. "Not a lot you can do with just a name."

"I called 411, but there's no listing for Satin Holiday." Drake scrubbed the inside of a greasy pan with a scouring pad.

"I hate to tell you this, man, but that sounds like a stripper's name." Damon laughed and slapped his brother on the back. "You better go look for her at the Gentlemen's Club."

"I know she's not a stripper."

"Chances are slim to none that you'll run into her again."

"I don't know. I have a feeling we might . . . meet again."

"You haven't been drinking, so what's up?"

"Wish I had an answer. I keep thinking about her and it's so strange because we didn't even have a conversation."

Damon poured dishwashing detergent into the dishwasher. "Is this love-'em-and-leave-'em-Drake talking?"

"I knew you would laugh."

"The only thing that can explain this crazy conversation is what you call love at first sight. Don't dis it, because that's what happened with me and Alanna. Here I was, ready to get into those Spelman girls' pants, and then I meet Alanna that first week. My playboy days were cut short."

"I'm not sure if your theory applies to my situation. When you and Alanna met, you couldn't stop talking to each other and you couldn't stand to be apart," Drake said, recalling their college days. "I didn't even get to talk to my mystery lady."

"Who else have you said that about? You usually complain because they won't leave you alone."

"You know how you wake up from a dream before it's finished? You try to go right back to sleep, but then you dream something else," Drake explained. "I just wonder how our conversation would have played out if we had a chance to talk."

"And you think you're going to get this chance again?" Damon asked in a have-you-lost-your-mind tone.

Drake gave his brother a thoughtful look. An honest answer would garner derisive laughter. But he wouldn't deny what he really wanted to believe. "I think so."

Laughing, Damon punched Drake in the center of his back. "Hey, alien, get out of my brother."

Four

The unexpected begets the unexpected

Satin and her two older brothers were gathered around their parents' dining room table eating dinner: roast beef, mashed potatoes, cabbage, macaroni and cheese, green beans, corn, and cornbread. Dessert waited in the kitchen—German chocolate cake and peach cobbler—to be devoured after dinner. As usual, Justin Holiday had already tasted the cake, hoping his mother wouldn't notice him eating dessert before dinner. But she always noticed and chided him. And Justin would smile with a guilty look on his face, and then shrug his shoulders. It was part of their Sunday-dinner ritual.

As was the dinner conversation about the week's highlights. There were few family secrets and they were never secrets for long. Confidences had a way of being intentionally and unintentionally revealed in between bites.

"Satin, did you ever hear about that job you interviewed for in Atlanta?" Justin asked.

"Atlanta!" Julia shrieked. "What job did you interview for? You never told me you went to Atlanta."

"Never mentioned it to me, either," Oliver Holiday

said, putting down his fork and piercing his daughter with an intense gaze.

Seeing the accusatory look on her parents' faces, a surge of guilt went through Satin. "I didn't tell—"

"Leave it to Justin to let the cat out of the bag," O.B. Holiday said.

"You knew about it, too?" Julia questioned, sending a disappointed glare in her firstborn's direction. Before O.B. could respond, she turned to Satin. "I can't believe you're thinking about leaving. Is Troy's job transferring him there? I never knew he wanted to leave. If you don't want to go, and I know you don't, tell him. I'm sure Troy will consider your feelings."

"Baby girl, I thought you just got a promotion on your job," her father said.

"You're asking too many questions at once." Satin wiped her mouth with a napkin. "I did interview for a job in Atlanta, but they never contacted me, so I guess I didn't get it."

"Thank God," Julia said.

"It's been over a month and they haven't called. Two weeks after that interview I was promoted."

"So you're not thinking about leaving?" her mother asked, relief on her face, even though worry rattled her voice.

"Why'd you go to the interview in the first place?" her father asked, a deep crease between his brows. "Atlanta . . . that's so far away from us."

"A headhunter called me about the job. It seemed like the perfect job, but I told her I wasn't interested in moving. She kept calling and finally I agreed to go to the interview just to see what it was about," Satin explained, without elaborating on an important detail—she really wanted the job. And every time she thought about the job, she thought about the smile man.

"I hope that recruiter lost your phone number," Julia griped. "If she calls again, tell her not to call you anymore."

"Well, I got my promotion. It came out of the clear blue sky and I'm happy with it."

"Baby girl is running things at her job," O.B. teasingly said. "You the man!"

"Wo-man," Satin said, giggling.

"She never told Troy about it," Justin said.

"You didn't tell Troy about your promotion?" her father queried.

"I told you," her mother said, "let the man be the man."

Satin shot Justin a mean look. "Why do you have such a big mouth?" Eyeing her parents, she said, "Troy knows about the promotion, but I didn't tell him about the interview in Atlanta."

"It's a good thing you didn't," Julia said. "You and Troy about to get married. No sense starting out a marriage with big decisions like that."

"Did you see Aunt Maggie when you were there?" Oliver asked, referring to his aunt.

"I didn't have time," Satin said. "I talked to her briefly on the phone. She was getting ready to leave for a doctor's appointment."

"Is she sick?" Julia asked.

"No, she was going for a checkup. She was in good spirits. She joked that going to the doctor was a normal part of being old."

"I'm glad Layla's there to keep an eye on her," Oliver said. "I know that no-good cousin of mine can't help much . . . except to try and take stuff from her."

"Don't get started with that," her mother said.

"I did drive over to see the land Aunt Maddie willed us."

"What do you mean us? O.B. and I aren't included,"

Justin said, reaching for a roll. "I don't understand it. I don't understand how she can get away with it."

"It was Aunt Maddie's land and she can do what she wants with it," Julia explained.

"It seems like discrimination to me. Maybe we should sue her estate." Justin looked at O.B. for support. "What was her problem anyway? Why did she hate men so much?"

"We've told you a million times," Julia said. "The man Aunt Maddie thought she was going to marry jilted her."

"Jilted. No one says that word anymore," Satin said.

"He didn't marry her because he was already married," added Oliver.

"That happened when she was twenty or twenty-one, right? Fifty years later she's still mad about it? So mad that she doesn't include any males in her will," Justin grumbled. "She just ices us?"

"She never gave us birthday presents or Christmas presents. Just the girls in the family," O.B. piped up. "So why are you so surprised she excluded us from her will?"

"How can you trip about something for fifty years? Some brother stands her up, so she hates men all her life. She never had sex again? Now that was her problem," Justin said. He caught the reproving glare on his mother's face. "Sorry, Mama. I'm going to get some dessert," Justin said, rising from his chair. "I say she was crazy."

"Who's that?" Julia said, upon hearing a car door slam.

"I'll go see," Justin went into the living room and peeked out the window. "More of Aunt Maddie's favorite nieces."

"The twins," Satin groaned, referring to Kendra and Keisha, her twin cousins who also inherited the land in Atlanta. "Kendra's been calling me every day, bugging me to sign the papers. "

"She's trying to buy a house and that money would be the down payment," Julia said.

"They knew you would be here," O.B. said.

Satin finished her drink. "They're going to be mad when I tell them I'm not signing yet."

"Why? Are you crazy like Aunt Maddie?" Justin asked. "Take the money and run."

"I like the idea of owning something," Satin explained. "I walked around on that land and my spirit told me not to sell it. Not yet, anyhow. I don't see what the big deal is. There's nothing around for miles and miles."

"Somebody must be interested in that property," her father said. "That's why they want to sell it."

"Satin thinks she got her forty acres and a mule," O.B. teased.

"I wouldn't put it like that, but I want to hold on to it. I'm thinking about getting an attorney to look over the papers."

"Why?" Julia asked. "Attorneys are expensive."

"Mama, I've learned from my job that you should always consult an attorney before you sign something."

The doorbell rang. Everyone looked around the table at each other, but no one moved.

"You want to go upstairs and hide before I answer the door?" Justin teased.

Satin shook her head. "If I try to hide, they'll tear up Mama's house looking for me."

"They know better," Julia said indignantly.

"I can't avoid seeing them." Satin stood. "I'll tell them my decision face-to-face."

"Aren't you getting big, bad and bold," remarked O.B. "Not the meek little mouse, no more."

"In case you haven't noticed, I haven't been little Miss Mousy for a long time."

"Satin, it wasn't that long ago that you were afraid to—"

Her hands planted, Satin glared at O.B. "To steal a title from some book I read in high school: that was then and this is now."

The doorbell rang again—a longer, insistent ring.

"I'll answer it," Satin said, leaving bewildered expressions on her family's faces as she left the room.

"Did you hear the news?"

The question broke Satin's concentration on the project milestone plan she was working on. She raised her eyes from the computer screen to meet the serious gaze of coworker Angela Johnson. "What news?"

"We're going to be bought." Angela stood in the doorway to Satin's office.

"That's old news," Satin said with a lackadaisical shrug. "I've learned not to take rumors seriously unless I hear it from PR or see it in the news."

"The news is from Linda Humphries. She's putting together a press release about it now."

"You're kidding," Satin said, disbelief in her voice. Linda Humphries was the director of public relations, the company's official communications point-of-contact. If she was writing a press release, that meant one thing—the rumor was a fact. "Vertical Visions is going to buy us?"

"Not them," Angela said, walking over to Satin's desk. "A different company. Visual Effects."

"Who are they?"

"They're owned by Ducent Technologies."

"This is serious."

"You're damn right it is. We're having a company meeting today at 2:00 P.M."

"Today?" Satin uttered.

"Check your E-mail."

Satin clicked on her E-mail window. She saw the bulletin blast, sent with a high-importance flag. "I've been so busy working on the milestone schedule, I haven't checked my E-mail."

"Forget that schedule. You need to start working on your résumé," Angela advised. "Your new title will definitely increase your marketability."

"Angela, you are jumping to conclusions."

Angela shook her head. "I don't think so."

"Maybe this new position will mean I won't get laid off, especially since no one has been hired for my old position."

"Wishful thinking, Satin. You better get your survival cap on," urged Angela.

"Don't be Miss Gloom and Doom. We don't know anything for sure. Merger or acquisition doesn't mean that everyone has to go."

"I'm not just speculating. I'm basing this on fact and previous experiences. Layoffs are brutal," warned Angela. "Update your résumé and get ready to hit the street."

"I'm not ready to throw the towel in just yet."

"I'll see you at the meeting," Angela said, before departing Satin's office.

Three hours later, Satin arrived fifteen minutes before the designated meeting time, but the room was already crowded with anxious-looking employees. It took her several minutes to locate a seat in the back of the room, near employees she didn't know. Their whispers echoed Angela's departing comment—*Update your résumé.*

The monthly meetings weren't unusual. The president of the company conducted monthly meetings in the large conference room to update employees on the company's performance and activities. New employees were welcomed, employees celebrating anniversary dates were acknowledged, and outstanding employees were rewarded with awards. It was a rah-rah session designed to keep employees motivated, excited, and energized about working there. The energy in the room, however, was far from festive and upbeat. Satin observed somber expressions, whispered conversations, and very little laughter.

Satin began to wonder if Angela's words would become prophetic.

She didn't have to wait long to find out. The president of the company didn't mince words or sugarcoat the situation. He immediately announced that a merger was in the works and that the company would be issuing a press release about it. "As a result, there will be a 30 percent reduction in the workforce due to overlapping responsibilities and roles. The reduction will happen immediately." The president further explained that affected employees would receive a generous severance package, and then he discussed the company's new direction and products.

Satin didn't believe she would be among the 30 percent. After all, she'd just been promoted and was recently involved in a successful product launch. And the president indicated that plans for product development and marketing would continue as scheduled.

At the meeting's conclusion, everyone slowly left the room whispering about the unexpected, disturbing news. Tears glistened in some employees' eyes. Satin engaged in conversation with other coworkers who concurred with her conclusion that her job was safe.

By the time she returned to her office, the workforce elimination process had begun. After witnessing the hasty and tearful departure of several coworkers, Satin closed her office door. Watching hardworking employees escorted to the door, their faces a mixture of anger and disbelief, was too painful to behold.

At 4:30 P.M., there was a knock on her office door. It wasn't a coworker rushing in to bid farewell and exchange phone numbers. It was her new boss. A big brown envelope was in his hand. A somber expression was on his face.

Satin didn't have to tell Troy that she had been laid off from her job. Word of mouth in East Cleveland spread news faster than a forest fire. When he found out from a mutual friend, he immediately tried to contact her.

Troy called Satin at home, but she didn't answer the phone. He called her cell phone, but voice mail was the response. So he went looking for her. First, he went to her apartment, but she wasn't there. He drove past her parents' house, but didn't see her sports utility vehicle. He called her friend Tyrece, but she wasn't there, either.

He redialed her cell phone and home numbers again, but she didn't answer. It was getting late, and each passing minute only increased his anxiety. He called her brother O.B., who informed him that he'd spoken to Satin earlier that evening. Worried, Troy decided to drive over to her apartment for the third time that evening. A sigh of relief came through his lips. Satin's car was in the parking lot.

Troy rang Satin's intercom number. She didn't answer so he pressed the intercom button a second time, hoping she would hurry. It was a bitterly cold night; the temperature had dipped below twenty-five degrees.

"Who is it?" she finally asked, after he rang the buzzer for the third time.

"It's me. Let me in."

"I'm not in the mood for company," Satin said.

"I'm not company."

"I have a pounding headache, Troy," she wailed, "and I just want to go back to sleep."

"Let me comfort you, baby."

"Troy, please. I had a terrible day."

"I know."

"Jerry told you?"

"Yes. I've been trying to reach you ever since," he impatiently said. "It's freezing out here." His voice became demanding. "Let me in!"

"I just want to be alone," she said in a desperate, sad voice.

"I won't—"

"You know how I feel when I have a migraine." Exasperation replaced desperation in her voice. "Just standing here and talking to you makes the pain worse."

"All right," he muttered, unable to hide his disappointment. "Go to bed and I'll come over tomorrow. I might be able to swing by at lunch."

"Okay," Satin said. "Good night."

Satin padded into the living room and lay down on the sofa. The room was dark, as it would be if she truly had a migraine. Her head wasn't pounding. She just didn't desire Troy's company. His presence wrought too many mixed emotions, and the layoff brought its own set of dark emotions.

She closed her eyes and dozed, listening to a classic soul radio station. An hour later she woke up; the radio station was playing an old song—"Your Smile" by Angela Windbush. The song was from the past but it didn't conjure up distant memories. The mysterious smile man appeared in her mind as the song's refrain repeated the words *your smile*. His question—"Is that your smile or the reflection of mine?"—replayed in her mind, bringing a tender smile to her lips.

"Your Smile" ended and a new song featuring the alto sax began to play. Satin listened to the music while pondering her future. The soaring sound of the saxophone mirrored the treble of her soul—crying for something more. She struggled with the restlessness in her spirit that was getting harder and harder to suppress.

Listening to the saxophone playing a higher, wailing cadence, she felt her restless spirit crying to be released: *I want more. I need more. I deserve more.*

Deciding to go to bed, she stopped in the kitchen for a drink of water and then went into her bedroom. She climbed under the covers and lay awake, thinking about tomorrow. What did the future hold? Should she ignore her spirit's cry? Before falling asleep, one question harbored in her mind: Was this the time to heed her spirit's call?

"Damn!" Leanne Miller swore furiously as she slammed down the phone. Stomping her foot on the floor, she flung herself facedown on the lavishly draped bed, bouncing on the lilac coverlet. Propped up on her elbows, she blew a corkscrew of blond hair out of her eyes. She was frothing mad and disgusted— her attorney had just revealed some devastating news: Her appeal was denied. Months of contesting her mother's will and she had nothing to show for her efforts, except very expensive attorney fees.

She didn't have the money to pay her attorney.

She didn't have the money to pay her taxes.

And her high-fashion boutiques were losing money. She needed to increase her boutique locations, advertise, and hire new designers. Everything she needed to do required money. Money she didn't have.

All because of Maddie Mae Holiday.

Leanne had loved Maddie, and even cried at the old woman's funeral. Maddie was the maid who took care of her and her siblings: cooking, cleaning, and tending to the family's needs. She had fond memories of Maddie—the woman had wiped her tears, mended her clothes, and brought special medicines when she was ill. She had been an intrinsic yet invisible member of the Mitchell household, but she never belonged. Everyone understood that.

Leanne's mother, Susan Mitchell, was a traditional Southern belle who understood the dividing line between the races—understood but seldom spoken. Susan frequently told Leanne that proper race relationships were maintained when blacks and whites clearly understood and stayed within their roles.

Yet her mother willed 25 percent of her estate to Maddie Mae Holiday.

Two bright crimson spots burned on Leanne's cheeks. "Do you know what you've done to me, Mama!" She sighed, rolling wearily over on her back. She stared up blankly at the shirred underside of the canopy, contemplating her options.

A voice suddenly said, "Morning," causing Leanne to jump up as though she'd been goosed.

"Graham!" she gasped, placing a hand over her wildly palpitating heart. "Goodness!" She stared at her lover through saucer-size eyes. "You frightened me! I didn't hear you come in."

"I know you were going to get that call today. I

thought you might need me." He leaned down and kissed her. "Looks like you got bad news."

"It was denied, just like the attorney said it would be." Her face changed from disappointment to concern. "But you shouldn't be here. Daniel might still have those detectives watching me."

"They haven't been watching for a while."

"This is too much to bear. The divorce and Mama's will. I can't deal with it."

"Yes, you can. You just have to calm down and think clearly. If you can't challenge the will, that means the estate can resolve things faster and begin paying more than your trust fund," Graham said, sitting on the bed. "You're still going to inherit a lot of money."

"I want all of it!" she cried, tugging on her hair.

"You tried, Leanne. But the judge wouldn't throw out the will. The sooner you stop fighting it, the sooner you'll get your money."

"But I still might not get the money right away."

"Why not?"

"I just remembered something my attorney told me a while ago. Maddie Mae bequeathed her estate to her relatives. Everybody has to sign some papers in order for the will to be fully executed. But not everyone has signed. Some developers are trying to buy some of Mama's land." Sighing, she plopped back down on the bed. "I don't know what pieces of land they want to buy."

"Back up a minute. Why haven't all the maid's heirs signed the papers?"

"I don't know. I really didn't care before because I didn't want them to get any of Mama's money."

"That's out of your control," Graham said. "You need to find out who won't sign the papers and why."

"The sooner the papers are signed, the sooner I get my money," Leanne said. "Not all of it, but—"

"It's still a lot of money," Graham said. "Feeling better?"

"Well, there's more you can do to make me feel better."

Graham smiled as he unbuckled his belt, feasting on Leanne. She was a classic golden girl: cornsilk hair, sharply etched cheekbones, and wide-set aquamarine eyes. Graham stripped off her nightgown and spread her legs, gently working two fingers up inside her.

"You get wet so fast." He grinned, sliding on a condom. His lips closed around her nipple, bringing it to its fullest and hardest.

Her blissful smile widened as she watched his tongue flick a moist, ticklish path over her sumptuous breast, and down the softly hollow of her belly to her blond-furred mound.

"To quote Scarlet O'Hara, 'I'll think about it tomorrow. After all, tomorrow is another day,'" she said, exaggerating her Southern drawl.

Graham laughed. "Remember the scene when he carried her up the stairs?"

"And she woke up deliriously happy and gleeful the next morning, completely oblivious as to the reason for her sunny mood," Leanne said.

"That's what I'm going to do to you," he said, entering her slowly.

"Hmm," she groaned, when he began to thrust with a very deliberate rhythm.

"Yes, tomorrow is . . . another day."

Five

A haircut, a broken engagement, a new direction

Satin greeted Tyrece with a bright, happy smile. "Hey, girl," she said, removing her full-length wool coat to reveal another layer of protective clothing: thick turtleneck, knit vest, and black wool pants. Two pairs of socks over stocking-covered legs inside her shoes shielded her feet from the weather. "It's freezing outside!"

"Freezing," Tyrece emphatically said. "And it's supposed to snow tomorrow."

"Possibly twelve inches. I'm sick of these long, cold dreary winters," she complained, sliding into the booth. "Have you been waiting long?"

"No, I just got here," Tyrece said, surveying the half-empty jazz club. In an hour it would fill up with the after-work, happy-hour crowd, and many would linger long after happy hour ended. "I haven't even ordered yet," she said, just as a waitress appeared at their table.

"What can I get you, ladies?" the waitress asked.

"I'll have a rum and Coke," Tyrece said.

"Mmm . . . I'll have the same."

"You're ordering a rum and Coke?" Tyrece said with disbelief. "You must be taking this layoff thing pretty hard. I know you were just promoted and it's disappointing to be out of a job, but you'll find something," she soothed, patting Satin on the back. "You're smart and—"

"Do I look worried? Did I come in here looking sad and blue?"

Tyrece tilted her head and assessed her friend's face. There was an unexpected glow in her brown eyes. "You did come in here smiling, like everything is normal. And you look . . . kind of excited."

"You know what they say: Life is change." A sanguine grin formed on Satin's lips. "Sometimes, change is good."

"That was a quick recovery," Tyrece said. "Yesterday, you were so devastated and hurt. You kept saying that you didn't think you would be one of the unlucky ones."

"I didn't think I would be. And I don't appreciate how they handled the situation." Her voice became indignant. "Just walked us out of there like we were calves being led to slaughter."

"Layoffs are never pretty," Tyrece remarked. "But I don't believe you're not worried."

Noticing a tall woman enter the jazz club, Satin said, "There's Brenda." They both waved at the woman.

"You don't have to pretend with me," Tyrece said in a tone of voice mimicking a psychologist. "You don't have to act like you're not worried about finding a job."

"I'm a little worried about finding another job." Satin inhaled and then slowly exhaled. "But I'm not worried about what I should do about the wedding."

Tyrece arched her brows. "What does that mean?"

Satin's eyes connected with Tyrece's. "I broke up with Troy."

"What?" Tyrece screamed, and covered her mouth when she realized her loud screech drew stares from other patrons in the club. "You broke up with Troy? Why?"

"Because . . . I don't want to marry him."

"Here you go, ladies," the waitress said, upon arriving with their drinks.

"Perfect timing," Tyrece said to the waitress. She turned back to Satin. "You just decided you didn't want to marry him. Something doesn't sound right."

"It was complicated because I was considering everyone's feelings and expectations but my own. Ever since he gave me the ring, I've felt really strange about the relationship. I started thinking about whether I loved him enough to be with him for the rest of my life." Satin sipped her drink, an introspective look on her face. "Forever is a long time. The thought of it made me sick."

"That's why you haven't made any wedding plans." Comprehension played on Tyrece's face. "I couldn't understand why you haven't even shopped for a wedding gown."

"I felt trapped. I didn't want to face the truth of my feelings. I lost my job and then something just clicked inside. Maybe it made me hear my inner voice. . . . I feel free to do what I really want."

"You're throwing too much at me," Tyrece said. "I understand the listen-to-your-inner-voice stuff. But when did you break up with him?"

"This afternoon."

"What happened?"

"Troy came over for lunch to console me about losing the job. He was trying to be sweet and considerate, and everything was fine until he said, 'Now you have time to plan a spectacular wedding.' He kept going on and on about the wedding. I had the strangest feeling in my heart. This little voice inside kept saying 'No, no, no.' It got louder and louder and then suddenly I screamed, 'No, no, no! I don't want to get married!'"

Tyrece's eyes enlarged. "What did he say?"

"He didn't hear me the first time. So I said it again."

"What did he do?"

"At first he didn't believe what he heard. He said, 'What did you say?' I told him I didn't want to get married. He gave me this weird look and his face transformed right before my eyes. He looked bewildered, then hurt, then mad."

"He was in shock," Tyrece said empathetically.

Satin nodded. "Then he walked to the door. I tried to give him the ring back, but he wouldn't take it. He opened the door, looked at me with the meanest expression on his face, and then left."

"He didn't ask for an explanation?"

"I don't think he wants to know why." Satin picked up her glass. "Or maybe he knows deep down inside, but didn't want to hear me say it out loud." She sipped her drink.

"I can't believe it," Tyrece gasped. "You're really serious?"

Satin nodded. "Yes."

"Maybe you're reacting to the layoff. Overreacting, that is."

"The layoff was the impetus, but it wasn't the reason." Satin reflected on her restless night. Sleep was intermittent, interrupted by uneasy dreams. "I had a dream last night about a wedding. I was all dressed in a wedding gown, but I was behind bars. I kept screaming, 'Let me out, let me out.'"

"What happened?"

"I don't know," she said, shrugging. "I woke up."

They were quiet for a few minutes, listening to the music.

"What are you going to do now?" Tyrece asked, breaking the silence.

"Move to Atlanta."

"Are you serious?"

"Yes, I'm serious."

"Your parents are going to be devastated."

"I know," Satin said. "I dread telling them."

Tyrece shook her head. "I don't want you to go, either."

"I know it's going to be hard to say good-bye to everyone, but my . . . spirit is telling me it's time for a change."

"Wait a minute. Did they call you about that job in Atlanta?"

"They haven't called."

"You're going to move there without a job?" Tyrece asked, her voice shrill with astonishment. "You've gone crazy."

"I always do what everyone thinks I should do. Maybe it's time for me to do something crazy. Maybe it's time for me to do what's right for *me!*"

Satin parallel parked in front of Dee's House of Style on Superior Avenue in East Cleveland. It took several tries before she angled her red Ford Explorer into the tight spot. She ignored the exasperated expression on the driver in the car behind her who anxiously waited for Satin to maneuver into the space.

She got out of the SUV and dropped several quarters in the meter, estimating that it would take two hours to get her hair done if Miss Dee was on schedule. But when she entered the salon and saw several women seated in the waiting area, she knew that Miss Dee was out of sync with her appointment book. Satin was disappointed, but not surprised.

Satin greeted some of the customers she knew and waved to Miss Dee.

"Hey, Satin," Miss Dee called from the rear of the shop. "I'll be right with you."

"Sure she will," an older woman mumbled.

"The day after tomorrow," another customer said. "Might as well make yourself at home."

"Oh, well," Satin said and took a seat. She conversed with the women about the weather, an upcoming formal ball, and the robbery of a local convenience store. Everyone grew silent when a woman's boyfriend came into the salon demanding money. After an awkward silence, conversation resumed only to be interrupted again when a rough-looking man came into the beauty salon selling CDs, perfume, and watches.

One hour later, Miss Dee motioned Satin to her chair.

"How you doing, Satin?" Miss Dee asked.

"Fine."

"I heard about the layoff." Miss Dee fastened a cape around Satin's neck. "I was sorry to hear about it."

Satin nodded at the woman who looked old enough to be her mother even though she was only ten years older. A big, dark-skinned woman, Miss Dee exuded warmth and motherly concern.

"You'll find something soon. Have faith and be strong. You're a smart girl and some company will snatch you up real quick like."

"I've already sent my résumé out," Satin said.

"Good, you're not wasting time being mad and sad. Besides, I wouldn't worry if I were you. Your family will take care of you," Miss Dee affectionately patted Satin's shoulders. "They ain't gonna let nothing happen to their baby girl."

"I'm twenty-seven. I'm not a baby." Satin gave Miss Dee an indignant look. "Everyone seems to forget that."

"I know you ain't a baby. But you the baby of the family. And the baby girl. Your family gonna take care of you. Ain't nothing wrong with that! Your daddy works hard at that Ford plant. Your mama ain't had to work in years. You're lucky, honey. Real lucky to have a family like that."

"I know I am," Satin said with mixed feelings, not wanting to discuss how her family's protectiveness affected her life. Many people would think she was ungrateful, but that was not the case. She was suffocating in their protective embrace. Now was the time to break out of their protective bubble and find out how lucky she was on her own.

"What can I do for you today?"

"I want a haircut."

"A haircut?" Miss Dee repeated in disbelief. "You mean a trim." Miss Dee removed the ponytail holder, freeing Satin's mane of long wavy black hair. She studied the ends of her hair. "You definitely need a trim."

Satin removed the folded magazine ad from the side pocket of her purse. "This is what I want." She handed the ad to Miss Dee.

"You want your hair like this?" Dee screeched, staring at the photo of a woman with a cropped bob. "Are you serious?"

"Yes!"

"You know how much hair I'll have to cut off?" Miss Dee tugged at Satin's hair and indicated with her hand where she would cut. Her hand was very close to Satin's scalp.

Satin nodded.

"That's all your hair."

"I know. I'm ready for a change."

"Let me see," said Terri, another hairdresser who worked in the booth across from Miss Dee. She stepped over to look at the picture. "That's a sharp haircut." Returning to her booth, Terri said, "It doesn't seem like something you'd like."

"I like that style. I always have," Satin said. "I just didn't have the nerve to wear it . . . until now."

"Your mama is going to be very upset," Miss Dee said.

"What about Troy?" Terri asked. "What is he going to say?"

"Troy has nothing to say about this!" Satin said in a defensive tone that dared them to question her no further. She observed the unspoken communication pass between Terri and Dee. Their faces were burning with curiosity. And Satin knew what they were thinking: *What did she mean about Troy? Did they break up?*

Terri and Miss Dee didn't probe. Gossip and rumors circulated in the salon, but the stylists usually let their clients do the talking. They knew when to listen to their clients and when to participate in their conversations. And the hairdressers knew they'd soon find out the reason for Satin's unexpected, out-of-character outburst.

"All rightie, then," Miss Dee said. "Sometimes a woman's got an itch for change." She gave Satin a reassuring smile, while deciding how to approach the haircut, envisioning how the cut would look on Satin. It would be a different look, a look that would highlight her beauty: the shape of her face, her high cheekbones, and her almond-shaped eyes. "It's going to look good on you."

Satin watched the hairdresser pick up the scissors and cut several inches of her hair. She closed her eyes, unable to watch. "Turn me away from the mirror."

"Okay," Miss Dee said, and spun the chair around so that Satin's back was facing the mirror.

Satin watched clumps of her hair fall to the floor. Long clumps of her pretty hair. Her stomach quivered and her heart raced. She was excited and frightened.

But there was no turning back. No, she didn't want to see the haircut in process. She preferred to see the results and behold a new woman in the mirror on the crest of change.

"Hi, Daddy," Satin said when she entered her father's workshop.

Oliver glanced up, his eyes leaving the nail he was hammering into the bookcase. Catching sight of Satin's new hairdo, he inadvertently hammered his thumb. "Damn," he muttered, rubbing his thumb, before placing the hammer on the workbench. "I almost didn't recognize you, baby girl. What you do with all your beautiful hair?"

Satin giggled. "Left it on Miss Dee's floor." She fluffed the longest piece of hair that draped over her forehead. "What do you think?"

Satin had closed her eyes when Miss Dee had spun Satin around to view the haircut in the mirror. She'd kept them closed until Miss Dee had urged her to open them. "You look beautiful, honey. Open your eyes." Satin had released a deep sigh and opened her eyes. A different woman stared back. An instant smile had formed on her face, a proud, approving smile.

Waiting now for her father to answer, she said, "Well, what do you think?"

"You're beautiful no matter what you do to yourself," he said, stroking his chin with his hand. "I kind of like it. It'll take some getting used to. What made you cut your hair?"

"I'm going through a metamorphosis."

"Am I supposed to go look for a dictionary? What are you talking about?"

"That's why I'm here. I have something to tell you."

"You got that serious look on your face. Sit down and tell me what's on your mind."

Satin sat down on the bench next to Oliver. She surveyed the work shed—her father's playground, his favorite place. She would miss moments like this, quiet moments with her father. Growing up, she'd spent a lot of time here, sometimes helping him, often times getting in the way.

"What's wrong?" Oliver inquired. "Is this about you and Troy?"

"Yes."

"You ain't pregnant, are you?"

Satin blushed, averting her gaze. "No." She paused, and then softly said, "I've decided to move to Atlanta."

Oliver's face had the grief-stricken look of a parent who lost a child to tragedy. This was the conversation he never wanted to have with any of his children, especially his only daughter. He dropped the nails in his hands. "You're not going to marry Troy?"

She shook her head.

"Why?"

"I don't . . . love him enough to marry him."

Oliver slowly nodded. A minute elapsed before he said, "You don't have to leave because you don't want to marry Troy."

"I want to leave."

"Who's going to look after you when you're sick? Who's going to fix your car if it breaks down? Who's going to repair things around the house?"

"I'll manage," she said, although his questions ignited some of the fears she suppressed. She'd decided to move forward in spite of those fears. "I'll be all right."

"You'll be alone and so far away from us. Here you know who to go see for different things. If there's a problem, I step in or Justin and O.B. handle it. You won't have that kind of support in Atlanta."

"Daddy, that's why I want to leave," she said with heartfelt emotion. "Everyone sees me as baby girl or Troy's girl or Justin and O.B.'s little sister. I want my own identity."

Frowning with confusion, he said, "I don't know what that means."

"I don't know if I know, either. I know I have to find out." Tears formed in her eyes. "I know I won't find it here."

Oliver squeezed Satin's hand. "We've just tried to protect you, baby girl. Make life easier for you."

"I know your intentions are good. But I feel like I'm suffocating. Oh, Daddy, it's so hard to explain. I want to do things on my own. I want to be truly independent. I want to know what I can do. I want to make it on my own." She wiped away the tears rolling down her face. "I've always liked Atlanta. We always had a good time when we visited in the summers. I have family and friends there, so I won't be completely alone."

"What about a job?"

"Remember I interviewed for that job in Atlanta . . ."

Oliver stared at Satin for a while as he came to the realization that there was nothing he could say or do to change her mind. There was something in her eyes that he'd never seen before—steely determination to chart her own course.

Sighing, he threw his hands up in resignation. "Let me know when you plan to leave. I'll take off work and drive down with you."

"Daddy, I'm leaving in three days. My stuff is already packed. I want to drive myself."

Aghast, his eyebrows shot up. "You've never driven that far by yourself."

"There's a first time for everything. If I get tired, I'll stop at a hotel."

"You can stop at Aunt Mary's house in Kentucky. That's on the way."

"Maybe. I really want to drive straight through."

"Why are you in a hurry? Are they rushing you to start right away?"

"Sort of," she said, not wanting to admit that that there was no job offer. Not at the moment. If she told him the truth, his fear would intensify her fears. "I know if I prolong leaving, you might talk me out of going by telling me about the bad, crazy world out there."

"It is a bad crazy world, baby girl."

"I know, Daddy." She kissed him on the top of the head. "I can take care of myself." In a firmer, more convincing voice, she said, "I *will* take care of myself."

"I know you will. I know you got it in you. You're a Holiday," he said, chuckling. "Are you going to stay with Aunt Maggie?"

Satin shook her head. "I'm going to stay with Zandra until I find an apartment and get settled."

"Zandra's an unusual girl, but I know she'll look out for you."

"I've worked up the courage to break up with Troy, get a haircut, pack up my things, and tell you I'm moving to Atlanta." She leaned her head on her father's shoulder. "But I think I'm running out of courage."

"You want me to tell your mother."

"Yes, please. She's going to be so mad and very sad at the same time. I'm afraid she'll talk me into staying."

Oliver squeezed Satin's hand. In spite of his misgivings, he understood her quest for independence. "I'll tell her," he quietly said, knowing how devastated his wife would be to learn that their only daughter was moving out of town. He would worry about them both for different reasons.

"Thank you, Daddy."

"I'm going to miss you, baby girl."

"Me, too." A fresh wave of tears rolled down her cheeks.

Chet's Neighborhood Bar and Grill was crowded. Some folks were regular Friday-night barflies. Some were weekend barhoppers. And some were there to bid farewell to Satin Holiday.

The bartender brought a round of drinks to Satin's table. "This is from the gentleman sitting at the end of the bar." The bartender placed drinks in front of Satin, Tyrece, and two other friends, LaTanya and Renee.

The women raised their glasses. Tyrece led the toast. "To Satin, my good friend who is bold enough to slay the fear monster."

"To slaying the fear monster," Renee said.

"Here, here," LaTanya said.

They clinked their glasses together and sipped their drinks.

"I didn't expect this," Satin said, observing the crowd of people there on her behalf.

"Now that you know how many people care about you, maybe you'll stay," Tyrece said.

"She can't," Renee said, nudging Satin. "She's slaying the fear monster."

Fifteen minutes later, the bartender brought Satin another drink. "Compliments of—"

"Martin Lewis," said a brown-skinned brother flashily dressed in a lime-green suit. "For the beautiful lady with the fly haircut." He stared at Satin as if she were an appetizer for lunch.

"Thank you, Martin," Satin said.

"Hello, ladies," he said to Tyrece, LaTanya, and Renee. Eyes on Satin, he said, "So you're leaving town."

"News spreads fast around here."

"Not as fast as word that you broke up with Troy," said Martin.

"It really isn't anyone's business," she said.

"What you don't understand is that many of us brothers have been waiting for a chance to get with you. Speaking for myself, as soon as I heard I started dialing your digits."

Satin remembered the unfamiliar numbers she'd seen scroll across her caller ID box. "Look, Martin, there's no sense in us having this conversation."

"If you wasn't leaving so quickly, there'd be plenty of reasons to have this conversation."

"How you going to step to Satin like this when you're living with Sheila Robinson?" LaTanya asked.

It's just a temporary thing," Martin said, waving his hand in a dismissive fashion. "I heard Troy wasn't too happy about the way you ended things," he said, taking a quick glance at the bar where Troy sat watching Satin.

"It's none of your business," Satin firmly said.

"I can understand where the brother's coming from. I'd be mad if my woman dumped me and then decides to move." Martin bent his head down close to Satin. "You got a boyfriend in Atlanta, don't you?"

"You need to go," Satin said in a commanding tone.

Martin lingered for a moment and then said, "I wish you the best in Atlanta. If you ever need me, call me."

"Who else is going to hit on you tonight?" Renee asked, referring to the bevy of brothers who expressed disappointment that Satin was leaving before they'd had an opportunity to pursue her.

"I feel like a commodity or something," Satin said.

"Must be nice to be wanted by so many men," Tyrece teased.

"If I was going to stay, I would date all of them," Satin joked.

"But I ain't feeling that vibe Troy is sending," Renee said. "He just staring at you like he wants to—"

"Hurt me or something," Satin said. "I've tried to talk to him, but he won't take my calls. He left me a message demanding that I never call him again. I can't believe he can just flip like that."

"It's his pride. I'm not saying that he's not hurt," Renee explained. "But you know the male ego. They can't take ego bruises."

"Considering the way he's looking at me," Satin said, "I'm glad I'm leaving town."

"When you get all settled I'll be down there to visit," Renee said.

"I'm coming, too," LaTanya said. "I'll be bringing my whole family."

Satin laughed. "Some of you will be sleeping on the floor."

"So how did your mother take the news?" inquired Renee.

"Daddy told her for me. She cried and ranted and cried and cried. But then she said something unexpected. Even though I lost the job first and then broke up with Troy, she said I was leaving because of Troy."

"Hmm. I thought your mother liked Troy," remarked Renee.

"She does. But she had a feeling that I wasn't crazy in love with him. She didn't want to say anything in case she was wrong, because she knew he'd be a good provider. I think she felt it was more important that I find a good provider, but deep down she's a romantic and she wants me to find that special one."

"I'll take money over love," Renee said.

"Me, too," LaTanya said.

"Girl, don't even try it, Miss-Love-To-Fall-In-Love,"

Satin said, smiling. Her smile faded when she noticed Troy coming toward them. "Troy's coming this way," she whispered.

When Troy walked past their booth, he made eye contact with Satin. The anger emanating from his eyes sent a shiver down Satin's spine.

"It's a good thing you're going to Atlanta," Tyrece said. "Troy looks like he wants to kill you."

"He has a temper," Satin said. "But he's never acted like this before."

"I'm going to miss you," Tyrece said, eyes welling with tears.

Tears instantly formed in Satin's eyes. "I thought I cried all my good-bye tears yesterday. Mama made dinner and it seemed like every relative in Cleveland was there."

"Did that make you want to change your mind?" La-Tanya asked.

"For a minute," Satin replied. "I know I'm leaving a lot of love and support. I know what's going to happen here. I don't what to expect in Atlanta. That's what's pulling me—the adventure of it all."

"I'm going to miss you, girl, but I have faith that you're going to be all right," Renee said. "You're smart, strong, and maybe you'll find that special somebody. The One."

"Let's toast to The One," LaTanya proposed.

"The one in me and the one for me," Satin said. "Here, here."

They tapped their glasses together.

Six

Satin begins the journey to her destiny

"Bye, baby girl."

"Drive safely."

"Make sure you keep the gas tank full."

"Going to miss you, little sis."

"Be careful of the men in Atlanta. I heard they're pretty wild."

"Don't let anyone slip anything in your drink."

"If you need money, baby girl, call me."

"Keep your cell phone charged."

"Don't talk to strangers."

"Call me if you need me. I'll be on the next plane."

"We'll be down there soon to check on you."

"Don't forget to give me your job number."

"What's the name of the company you're going to work for?"

"The roads are clear now, but if it starts to rain hard, pull over."

Words of love, words of concern, words of worry—spoken from their hearts. Words spoken before her family bid Satin farewell and she got into her Ford Explorer for the twelve-hour drive to Atlanta. Words filled with tears—shed and unshed.

Satin managed to drive without crying for the first

few hours. But when she passed Cincinnati, her vision became blurred. Not just by the rain hitting the windshield. Big raindrops splattered against her window, calling out the stormy emotions she held within. Scattered raindrops turned into a rush of rain as the clouds unleashed a torrential downpour. The tears she valiantly tried to contain began to fall, hitting the steering wheel. She wiped the tears away. A futile effort as more tears came, like the rain in the sky, seemingly endless. She refused to pull over and wait for the rain to stop.

Nothing was going to stop her from reaching her destination.

Either the rain would stop or she'd eventually drive past the rain, just as she would have to ride out the storm in her heart. She didn't let her tears make her stop and turn back in the opposite direction. She didn't let the sadness of the emotionally draining farewell deter her from her mission. She didn't let the insidious fear of being alone and unprotected overtake her senses. She didn't let the specter of the unknown—the future—overwhelm her.

She kept driving.

Through the rain.

Through her tears.

Through the storm of her emotions.

She drove through Kentucky and into Tennessee. Her cell kept ringing: Her father called, her mother called, her two brothers called, her friends called. Sometimes she had to clear her throat before answering, not wanting to reveal her emotional state. Satin knew they weren't fooled; they pretended to believe that she was all right, because that's what Satin wanted them to believe.

Getting closer to Georgia, she called Zandra.

"I still can't believe you're really coming," Zandra said. "If you're in Tennessee, you're almost here."

"The sign said 197 miles. That's about four hours."

"The last hour is always the longest," Zandra said. "But you'll be here soon. I'm so excited."

"That gives me plenty of time to think about job hunting. I've sent my résumé to some headhunters and responded to some online job ads. I've had two calls from headhunters who want to interview me. I even have an interview set up for next week."

"Child, you are not going to have a problem finding a job. Especially with your skills. And you know I have some big-time contacts. I've sent your résumé to a couple of folks."

"Thanks. I have some money, but I don't want to use up my savings. I'll be busy job hunting."

"You'll be busy, all right. You'll have a job very soon and you even have a party to go to next week."

"A party?"

"A cocktail party. Some of ATL's movers and shakers will be there."

"I don't know. I need to concentrate on looking for a job, so I can get an apartment."

"How about concentrating on having some fun? That's one of the reasons you left Cleveland."

"Reason number five."

Zandra laughed. "What are reasons one through four?"

"I'll tell you later—I have another call," Satin said. "Probably Mama calling for the fifth time."

"Call me when you get to my exit. I'll meet you at the gas station. I don't want you getting lost."

"I'm not going to get lost."

"Girl, you always get lost. You know you have the get-lost gene. You can't help it."

"I rebuke that gene. I'll be ringing your doorbell in a few hours."

"After you call me from around the corner."

"I'll bet you dinner I'm not going to get lost," Satin said, before pressing the button to connect with an incoming call. "Hello."

"This is Randall Cunningham from VoiceBox. Is this Satin Holiday?"

Satin's heart jumped and she almost dropped the phone. "Speaking."

"I'm calling about the product manager position you interviewed for some time ago."

"Yes."

"Are you still interested in the position?"

"Yes, I am."

"We'd like to make you an offer."

A wide grin spread across her face. She didn't scream her immediate thought: *So you didn't hire the brother with the melt-your-heart smile.*

Satin got off at the next exit and pulled into a gas station. This conversation was something to stop for— it was part of the destination. Maybe, she thought, it was a sign of destiny.

"You made it!" Zandra exclaimed when she opened the door and saw road-weary Satin standing there. She welcomed her with a tight embrace. "I'm so glad you're here."

"Me, too," Satin said, walking into Zandra's three-bedroom apartment. After leaving two suitcases in the hall, she plopped on the sofa. "I feel like I'm still moving. That was the longest drive of my life."

"You did it, girl. You made excellent time and you didn't get lost."

"I told you I deep-sixed that get-lost gene."

"Tell me your secret. I'd like to deep-six my fat gene. I say that as I think about food. I owe you dinner. Want to order some Chinese?"

"I'm starved. Let me rest a few minutes and then I'll unload the car."

"Don't worry about it. I'll have Mike and Matthew do it. They'll be happy to."

"Sure they will," Satin said sarcastically.

"I told them that you were coming and they volunteered to help," Zandra said. "They're my friends. They're cool people."

"I'm too tired to protest."

Hours later, the scented water in the marble Jacuzzi bubbled as Satin slid into black tub. Closing her eyes, she rested her head on a black shell cushion, her fertile mind doing quantum leaps.

I have a job!
I'm in Atlanta!
I have a job!
I'm in Atlanta!

Overjoyed by thoughts of tomorrow, she didn't think about what she'd left behind: the safety net of family and the security of familiar surroundings. The future, once so far away, was now. It felt as surreal as an Alfred Hitchcock movie.

Her mind leaped from the surrealism of the moment to the unfolding reality of her life to the probability of seeing the man with the melting-pot smile. He seeped into her mind as soon as she'd received the phone call from Randall Cunningham. The truth of the matter was that he'd never left her mind. With just a wisp of a conversation, he'd somehow whittled his way into her subconscious.

She couldn't fathom the reason for his mysterious presence. Luxuriating in the warm water, she stilled herself, so that she could hear her inner voice. There, she would find the answer. If not now, then later.

Seven

Haunted by Satin's serendipitous smile

Drake's home office was on the main level of his two-story home in an upscale subdivision near Cascade Road in southwest Atlanta. He frequently worked at home before going to work or late at night. His office was no different than the rest of the house—decorated in ultracontemporary furniture and unusual colors like crimson red, purple, and yellow. An eclectic collection of artwork hung on the walls: a Romare Bearden, a William Tolliver, an Ernie Barnes.

Hunched over his computer, he lifted his gaze to view the faceless people in the painting above his desk. Giving in to the feeling of distraction, he laced his fingers together behind his head against the high-back leather chair and let his mind wander. It wasn't the report that drew his attention from the computer screen to the colorful painting. It was the face of an unknown woman, the smile of a woman named Satin Holiday. A smile that haunted him and a name that seemed to appear in the most innocuous of places.

Drake opened a Victoria's Secret catalog and casually flipped to a page boasting a new line of lingerie. Neither the scantily clad women nor the sexily designed underwear or unusual color palette sparked his interest. It was the name of the new line, The Satin Collection, that affected him, conjuring the memory of her face.

Several days ago, Brent Norwood presented ideas for a communications program that they were launching for a Fortune 500 company. Brent was full of excitement and energy as he described the visual elements of his design concept: "The collateral will have a satin finish for a look of sophistication and high impact."

Satin. That word again. Her face reappeared in his mind. Her beautiful brown eyes, beguiling smile, and that little mole near the corner of her lip.

And there was the overnight box sent by the interior decorator he'd hired to work on his house. Samples of wallpaper were inside, along with a note from the interior decorator recommending the red-striped satin wallpaper for his bedroom. That word again—*satin*—but wrought with new meaning.

How he wished he had another opportunity to meet her. Although he didn't know what he'd do if that wish came true, he knew that he wouldn't repeat is-that-your-smile-or-the-reflection-of-my-smile? line. He cringed every time he thought about it. His only comfort was that she thought his opening line was somewhat original.

Perhaps he should have used the pick-up lines women used on him. He'd heard plenty, but responded to few. Some of the women's lines were original, but the women were not. They were indistinguishable, but there was something original about Satin Holiday. He felt the uniqueness of her being when she smiled and when their eyes met again as she'd passed by his client's office. For a brief second, he considered interrupting his presentation to go out and properly introduce himself. It was a fleeting thought, disappearing as it entered his mind. A snippet of a moment that was gone before either realized that something significant had happened. If such a moment happened again, he wouldn't let it pass unnoticed.

Sighing, he returned to the reality of the moment—reviewing the concept designs that would be presented to VoiceBox Communications—the company where he'd briefly met Satin.

The doorbell suddenly rang. Drake went into the hall and peeked through the peephole, surprised to see his sister-in-law standing on the other side of the door.

"Alanna," he said, upon opening the door.

"We thought we'd surprise you," Alanna said.

"We?" Drake questioned.

"Boo!" His ten-year-old niece, Lane, jumped out from behind her mother.

"Boo to you!" Drake kissed Lane on her forehead, and then stepped to the side. "Come on in."

Lane rushed through the front door. "You got anything to eat? I'm hungry."

"You just ate," Alanna admonished.

"An hour ago," Lane said, going into the kitchen, followed by her mother and Drake.

"Help yourself to whatever you like," Drake offered while opening the refrigerator. "Want some pizza?"

"Is it Pizza Hut or Domino's?" Lane asked, her hands planted on her narrow hips.

"What difference does it make if you're so hungry?" Drake asked, staring at his niece's cute face. Dressed in denim overalls, her hair was a beautiful patch of long braids.

"This girl is so picky," Alanna explained. "She only likes Pizza Hut pizza."

"I wonder where she got that from," Drake wryly commented.

Wearing an engaging grin, Lane said, "Your big brother."

"You know where everything is, Lane. Help yourself." Drake turned to Alanna. "Are you starving, too?" he asked, levity in his voice.

"No," she answered with a half smile.

"Want something to drink?"

"I'll take some wine."

"Go have a seat in my office and I'll bring some in."

"Okay," Alanna said before leaving the room.

Lane placed two slices of pizza on a plate. "Mommy wants you to help plan Daddy's birthday party."

"Oh, yeah. I forgot Damon's birthday is coming up."

"And—"

Drake removed two wineglasses from the kitchen cabinet. "And what?"

"I think she has something serious to talk to you about," Lane said while putting her plate of pizza in the microwave.

"Why do you think that?" Drake asked, pouring wine into the glasses.

"She's worried that Daddy might lose his job."

"I didn't know about that."

Lane covered her mouth with her hands. "I probably wasn't supposed to tell you that."

"Find something on TV to watch. No BET or MTV videos, okay?"

"Okay." Lane removed the pizza from the microwave. "Uncle Drake, when are you going to give me a ride on your motorcycle? I want to go real fast."

"When your mommy and daddy give their consent."

"Daddy says it's okay."

"But your mother says no."

Lane rolled her eyes. "She's so overprotective."

"That's her job," Drake explained. "One day you'll appreciate it."

Lane moved closer to Drake. Lowering her voice, she said, "We don't have to tell her."

"Lane, don't even think about it," he firmly said. "And don't try to do stuff behind your mother's back. That's not very nice, so don't think like that."

"Okay," she said in a disappointed voice.

Drake went into his office and found Alanna resting her head against the sofa arm. Worry was etched on her face. He handed her a glass of wine. "So Damon thinks he's going to get laid off. Don't worry, Alanna. He'll get another job."

"Lane has big ears and a big mouth." Alanna sipped her wine. "I'm worried that he may get hit, but we'll deal with it."

"Do you think we'll be able to surprise Damon this year?"

Alanna chuckled. "It's going to take some planning and maneuvering."

"Maybe we should tell him that we're not going to have a party. Just tell him we're going to take him out to dinner."

"And have the party after dinner," she said, smiling. "We might be able to surprise him like that." They spent the next fifteen minutes discussing the details of Damon's party.

"What's wrong?" Drake asked after a moment of silence.

She brought the glass to her mouth, bringing her wedding ring into Drake's line of vision. He remembered loaning his brother money so he could purchase an engagement ring for Alanna. He often thought that loan was the best investment he ever made, as his brother had a successful marriage.

That thought led to the memory of his fateful wedding day. Alanna broke the news to him that Tavia wasn't going to walk down the aisle. Alanna and Tavia were friends, and Tavia had called Alanna from the airport. Alanna almost cried when she told him about

Tavia's decision; his devastated reaction was the only reason she held back her tears. In that dark moment, a bond formed between them, a bond that respected her marriage to his brother and her friendship with Tavia.

Alanna rose from the sofa and walked to the doorway. She didn't see Lane lurking nearby. She shut the door. "I don't want Lane to hear this," she said, returning to the sofa.

Fear suddenly pricked Drake's skin. "What's going on?"

"Something's wrong with me. I have to get some tests done."

"Is it serious?" he asked in a gentle tone.

"I hope not," she whispered, sadness claiming her face.

The burly, wide-necked sales representative assessed Drake when he pulled into Mike's Motorcycles driving a black convertible Jaguar. He tapped his associate's shoulder. "Looks like we gots us a customer," Jim-Bob said with a grin as wide as his girth.

Ray looked up from the sports section of the *Atlanta Times*. "Time to make some money." Eyeing Drake get out of his car, Ray said, "He probably don't know a gasket from a engine."

"Sometimes those are the best customers," Jim-Bob said.

"I betcha five dollars he don't know nothing about bikes," Ray challenged.

Jim-Bob watched Drake inspect the bikes on the lot. "You sure you want to place a bet like that? You owe me five dollars from last week."

"I'll pay you on Friday when we get paid. I always pay up what I owing."

"You going to owe me ten dollars. I think he might know a thing or two about bikes."

Jim-Bob walked over to Drake. "Good afternoon, sir. How can I help you today?" He extended his hand. "My name is Jim-Bob."

Shaking the white sales rep's hand, Drake introduced himself. He surveyed the showroom, impressed with the display of bikes. "I'm looking for a Harley-Davidson Heritage, the anniversary edition."

"You came to the right place," Jim-Bob said to Drake, and then grinned at Ray. "You're 0 for 2."

"Yeah, yeah, yeah. Sometimes you win and sometimes you lose," Ray said, while walking away. "Excuse me. I gotta take a leak."

"Sorry about that. Ray just don't what to say in front of customers," Jim-Bob said,

Drake gave Jim-Bob a curt nod, noticing the sales rep's profile was like a wind-eroded boulder. Heavy brows, the nose wide and disfigured, the chin like an unspoken challenge. It looked like a face that been punched at different times.

Jim-Bob pointed to the bike near him. "Let me tell you about this bike," he said, and began describing the bike's features.

"Impressive," Drake said.

"When are you wanting to buy?"

"It depends on when I find something I like."

"If you ain't in a real hurry, Kawasaki is going be shipping out their new models."

"I didn't think they were building new models until next year."

"This is a special edition. You want to see a picture?"

"Sure."

"I got one right here," Jim-Bob said, stepping over to his desk. He rummaged through the drawers before finding the picture. "Here it is!" Jim-Bob held up the picture for Drake to see. "It's got a strange name: Satin Divine."

Drake peered at the picture and then began to laugh. There was her name again. It was unbelievably uncanny how her name—in different contexts—kept appearing. It was as if he were being dared to forget her. Or was the dare that he couldn't forget her?

Drake's full-throttle laugh brought a confused expression to Jim-Bob's face. "Sir, maybe you ain't understand me."

"I'm laughing because the name is incongruous with the way the bike looks."

Jim-Bob laughed even though he didn't understand what Drake meant. He didn't want to alienate a customer on the hook.

"That name just doesn't fit that bike," Drake explained. "With that type of engine, it should be called the Speeding Bullet."

"Oh, yeah," Jim-Bob said, laughing heartily. "It got heavy engine power, that's for sure."

"When will the bikes be in?"

"It's a custom order, but Mike, the owner, ordered one for himself and maybe two or three more. Man, he got over fifteen bikes. I can find out when the bikes are coming in. I'll give you a call and let you know."

"All right," Drake said, opening his wallet and removing a business card. "You can reach me at this number."

"I'll be a-calling you real soon."

Drake left Mike's Motorcycles with an unexpected rush of euphoric clarity: He was going to see Satin Holiday again. He didn't how or when, but there had to be a reason why her name kept revealing itself to him.

Eight

Humming to the jazz music playing on her car's radio, Satin exited from Interstate 20 onto Ashby Street. She turned right, heading away from Atlanta University Center toward Aunt Maggie's house. It was mid-February but felt like springtime: It was leave-your-jacket-in-the-car warm. It was midday. People were walking along the sidewalks and cars were speeding through intersections. There was a familiarity about the area reminiscent of Cleveland: The faces were varying shades of brown, there were dilapidated storefronts next to renovated or new buildings, young girls were holding babies on their hips, groups of brothers huddled together, people standing at the bus stop.

So much the same, yet somehow different, Satin thought while pulling into the carport of her aunt's house. Lovingly tended flower beds bordered the small yard, reminding Satin of Aunt Maggie's frequent warnings: "Stay out of the front yard. Don't trample my flowers."

The thirty-year-old ranch-style house was better maintained than most, but some of the cars on the street were probably worth more than the house. Satin walked around to the front door, passing a large bay window. As she walked up the steps, the door opened.

"I thought that was you," Aunt Maggie said, greeting her great-niece with a tight hug and a kiss on the cheek.

"It's so good to see you, Aunt Maggie." Satin inhaled the scent of lavender perfume her aunt had worn as long as she could remember.

"Now that you're officially here, welcome to Atlanta, honey."

Satin returned her aunt's warm smile. "It's good to be here."

"Come on in. I fixed you some lunch."

"Aunt Maggie, you didn't have to do that. I didn't want to trouble you." Satin wasn't hungry, but wouldn't dare hurt her aunt's feelings by turning down her hospitality.

"Ain't no trouble. You know I love to cook. I miss having folks to cook for," she said while walking into the kitchen. "Have a seat and let me fix you a plate."

"Yes, ma'am." Viewing her aunt's face, Satin concluded that she'd aged gracefully. Her skin was still smooth, with only a few wrinkles betraying her seventy years. Her eyes were calm, reflecting the nature that remained through years of life's many ups and downs. Her gray hair waved gently to her shoulders. "You look wonderful, Aunt Maggie."

"I try to keep myself busy. I'm at the church almost every day." She placed a plate filled with greens, tomatoes, macaroni and cheese, and fried chicken in front of Satin.

"Thank you," Satin said, the aroma stimulating her taste buds.

"Would you like some tea?"

"Yes, ma'am. I've always loved your tea. It's so sweet and delicious. I don't get tea like that at home."

"You have to boil the tea for exactly six minutes and then you put in plenty of sugar," Aunt Maggie explained. "Plenty of sugar."

Aunt Maggie went to the kitchen cabinet, retrieved a glass, and then poured iced tea into it. As she placed the glass on the table, she said, "You cut your hair. That's what so different about you."

"Yes, ma'am. I can't believe I did it, either." Satin sipped her tea. "But I wanted a change."

"Change is good sometimes. It's very becoming on you. Makes me think of that movie star. What's her name? She lived here for a while. She was married to a baseball player who used to play for the Braves."

"Halle Berry. Everyone says that."

"Let me tell you something: You're prettier than her." Aunt Maggie pinched Satin's cheek.

Satin chuckled. "This is delicious."

"Have you seen Layla yet? She was so excited when she heard you were moving here."

"We're going to have lunch," Satin said.

"We're planning a party for you. A welcome-to-Atlanta party. All your aunts and uncles and cousins will be there."

"Aunt Maggie, you don't have to do that. I don't want all that attention."

"It's already in the works, honey. We just need to decide on a date." Aunt Maggie poured herself a glass of iced tea and sat down at the kitchen table.

"I start my job next week. How about the following week?"

"I'm going on a women's retreat with the church," Aunt Maggie said. "We can have the party the following week."

"Okay." Satin dabbed her mouth with a napkin. "Maybe I'll come visit your church one Sunday."

"Oh, you must come. And you'll want to join," Aunt

Maggie said with conviction. "They have a lot of activities for single folks. You can meet you a nice young man to marry."

"Oh, I'm not really interested in men right now."

"Well, I thought since the fellow you was engaged to broke up with you—" Aunt Maggie gave Satin a chiding look. "Now don't be like Maddie. Don't pine your life away over a man."

"Aunt Maggie, I broke up with him," Satin said with a hint of humor in her voice. "I'm the one who didn't want to get married."

Shocked, Aunt Maggie placed her hands against her cheeks. "You did the jilting?"

"It wasn't quite like that. We hadn't even set a wedding date."

"That kind of thing can really affect a person for a long time." Her brows deeply furrowed, Aunt Maggie asked, "Why didn't you want to marry him?"

A cloud flitted across Satin's picture-perfect features. "I didn't love him the way a wife should love a husband. Believe me, I'm not pining my life away. I don't hate men. I hope to find someone I can really fall in love with. "

"Maddie loved that man so much, she couldn't love another. I don't think she really hated men as much as she was afraid of getting hurt again."

"What happened?" Satin asked. "I've heard all kinds of stories, but what really happened?"

"Maddie was supposed to marry Wilbur Jenkins. They were going to get married by the justice of the peace. But Wilbur didn't show up. She was powerfully hurt," Aunt Maggie explained. "She waited for hours, but he never came. We found out later that he had another family."

"He didn't live here?"

"No," Aunt Maggie said, shaking her head. "He was

a porter for the railroad. Atlanta was a major stop back then. Maddie met him when she took the train to visit our cousins in Tennessee."

"I never knew this," Satin said.

"Maddie would get so excited when he came to town. And when he asked her to marry him, she was glowing like a lightning bug." Aunt Maggie chuckled at the memory. "She was going to travel the world with him and have an exciting life."

"But she never recovered when he didn't marry her," Satin said, feeling more empathy for Aunt Maddie than she ever felt before. The stories she'd heard were unflattering and portrayed Aunt Maddie as an eccentric, bitter woman who rarely smiled. Now she understood the moment in time that lasted a lifetime.

"She wouldn't let anybody court her. Some nice fellows came a-calling, but Maddie wouldn't give them the time of day," Aunt Maggie said. "She worked in a laundry for a time, and then she started working for the Mitchell family. Worked for them until she died."

"Did she ever see him again?"

"I can't say," Aunt Maggie said, remembering the tortured words whispered by her dying sister. Although Maddie hadn't requested that she keep her revelation a secret, Maggie assumed that she'd want her secret to remain such. "She never forgot him. Spoke his name before she died."

"Wow! I can't imagine loving someone like that," Satin said, though that was the kind of feeling she longed for. Satin wondered how she would react if she experienced such a feeling and then lost it.

"Eat up," Aunt Maggie said, rising from the table. "Your food is going to get cold."

"Yes, ma'am." Satin picked up her fork and ate some of the macaroni and cheese.

While Satin finished eating, Aunt Maggie cleaned

up the kitchen after refusing Satin's offer to help. She returned several bottles of seasonings to the spice rack and cleaned the countertops and stove. She neatly folded a washcloth under the kitchen cabinet. "Now, how come you haven't signed your name on those papers them lawyers done sent everybody?"

"I don't know, Aunt Maggie," Satin said, shrugging. "I don't have a real reason, other than I like the idea of owning land."

"That sounds simple enough, but it's creating some problems for your cousins."

"That's not my intention at all. The twins have been bugging me, especially when they doubled the offer. Before I left, they practically begged me to sign those papers."

"They're not the only ones who want you to sign the papers."

"What do you mean?"

"This developer came around here a couple of weeks ago. I guess he thought I could do something since I'm Maddie's twin."

"I drove out there. There's nothing around for miles. It doesn't look like anything worth developing."

"Honey, Atlanta is growing by leaps and bounds. Folks living in places that wasn't around when I was a girl. Black folks moving into parts that blacks wouldn't dare move to years ago," Aunt Maggie explained. "It might be an area that they expecting to grow into something. That land might be nothing but grass and weeds now, but some big-shot developers got their eye on turning that land into something that makes money."

"I never considered that," Satin said with a thoughtful gaze.

"Let me find that man's card. Maybe you should talk to him," Aunt Maggie said before leaving the kitchen. Satin had already finished her food and was washing the plate when Aunt Maggie returned. "I forgot where I put it," Maggie said, placing the card on the table.

Satin read the name on the card: Jacob Murphy. "I guess I'll call him and see what all this is about."

5555 Peachtree Road.

The elegant white letters, outlined in black, graced the creamy whipcord canopy that extended from the building to the street. Engraved plaques, shiny as new money, repeated the four-digit number on either side of the brass and etched-glass doors.

The sign had escaped Satin's attention when she'd interviewed, but on her first day of work, she viewed her surroundings from a different perspective. After all, she was going to be coming through those doors every day.

When she entered the reception area, her mind replayed the moment she looked into the face of the brother with a smile that haunted her. Now she was in the very place where the moment had become a memory. But the déjà vu was incomplete: The handsome stranger wasn't there.

Satin noticed the visitor's log, and wondered if his name was recorded there. She knew the date of their visit, but not his name. She'd have to weed through the signatures, narrowing it to the signature that appeared next to hers. The only way to find out would be to ask the receptionist if she could examine the visitor's log.

If only I could be that bold and outrageous, she thought. Outrageous behavior wouldn't make a good first impression, so she requested to see her new manager. "Randall Cunningham is expecting me," Satin informed the receptionist.

"Okay. Just sign in and I'll call him," the receptionist said, pressing buttons on her phone.

Satin signed her name in the visitor's log, realizing

that it was her opportunity to scan through the other signatures. It was the right opportunity, but definitely not the right time. The receptionist would notice if she flipped back through the log. Another thought occurred: *What will I do if I see his name?*

The receptionist hung up the phone after speaking to Randall Cunningham. "You didn't have to sign in. You're an employee. Welcome to VoiceBox, Satin Holiday."

"Thanks," Satin said, returning the receptionist's friendly smile.

"Randall will be right down."

By the time Satin sat down on the sofa, Randall appeared in the lobby. "Hello, Satin. It's good to see you. I'm glad you decided to join our organization."

"I'm glad to be here."

"Let me show you your office and give you a chance to get settled."

Satin's office wasn't impressive. It was rather small and the furniture was old. While organizing her desk, the office manager gave Satin an office-supply catalog so that she could order new furniture and office accessories.

Later, during a brief meeting with Randall, she learned about the company's latest business plans. "I'll leave these materials for you to read," Randall said. "Also, I've arranged for you to meet with the technical team so that you can see the product for yourself."

"That'll be great," Satin said. "When?"

"Tomorrow morning," Randall answered. "How do you feel about going to a meeting with me this afternoon?"

"Sure. Who with?"

"Marketing Missions, an ad agency, will be coming in to present their ideas for a marketing campaign."

"That should be interesting."

"We'll be meeting in the Mars conference room at three o'clock." Observing her curious expression, Randall elaborated, "All the conference rooms are named after the planets of the universe."

"I'll be there."

Satin spent the rest of the morning reviewing the product specification materials. She activated her E-mail and voice mail accounts and read about the company's products on their Web site. Navigating their Intranet site, she gained insight into the company culture.

The company's dress code was business casual, but Satin had opted to wear a business-inspired black suit for her first day on the job. She headed to the Mars conference room ten minutes early and found the room empty. After a quick eye sweep of the room, she advanced on the nearest of the twelve identical gilt wood chairs surrounding the eight-foot-long conference table. She placed her pad and pen on the table, and was admiring the planet-themed artwork on the wall when Randall entered with three people from Marketing Missions. He introduced the art director, copywriter, and managing partner. She had never seen the creative director or the copywriter. But she'd seen the managing partner before—in the lobby on the day of her second interview.

"Hello," she said, shaking the hand that belonged to the smile man. The touch of his hand was electric; she forced herself not to respond to the shock. And when she met his gaze, she felt trapped in that instant of contact of seeing nothing else. Satin forced herself to blink, to return from the blind impact of his heart-touching stare. A stranger to her eye, but not her heart.

"Very nice to meet you, Satin Holiday," he said in a voice that made her think of James Earl Jones.

His touch was powerful. There was no pressure, but Satin felt the response shoot through her as though their bodies, rather than their hands, had pressed together. She smiled at him and then suddenly laughed.

"Have you two met before?" Randall asked.

"Not formally. I saw him in the lobby when I interviewed with the vice president. And later, when I was leaving, I saw him in your office." Satin paused, self-consciously aware that everyone was staring at her. "I thought he was interviewing for my job."

Everyone laughed as they took a seat at the conference table.

"That's a funny story," Randall said. "Drake's our new ad man. We signed with his agency because we want a new look for our collateral. As I said, Satin's our new product manager, so you guys will be working closely together."

Sitting across the table, Drake couldn't help staring as he compared his memory of her loveliness with the reality of her beauty. She'd cut her hair. The long waves of hair he'd imagined touching was gone. The haircut accentuated her long, slender neck. Somehow she was even more beautiful than he remembered. Her skin was a lovely golden brown. Her brown eyes sparkled with intelligence. Her mouth was sensuously wide. And there was that Marilyn Monroe mole near her lips. Simple diamond earrings adorned her ears.

Satin's scrutiny started with the lips that curled into an unforgettable smile. Her heartbeat kept increasing as she stared at the masculine beauty of his face that reminded her of a darker-skinned version of Shemar Moore. She tried not to look into those gray eyes but couldn't help staring into them, and getting lost inside his depthless gaze—again.

Fighting her way back to the moment, Satin focused on Randall's marketing plans and strategies. Conscious of her hands fidgeting in her lap like some trapped, high-strung animal, she forced herself to still them and struggled to regain a semblance of professional decorum.

Randall's marketing spiel didn't filter through her thoughts about Drake. She half listened to his plans for a phased-approach marketing strategy, but had to think fast when Randall solicited her opinion.

Satin cleared her throat. "I think it will be an effective way of getting consumers' attention and allows us to take advantage of the momentum built by the competitor."

Drake smiled at Satin as a proud father would at his child's school play. He'd sensed she had paid little attention, as they took turns staring at each other. Yet she rebounded with an intelligent response. Beauty and brains. He'd met many black women with such a combination. Invariably, he found too much beauty, not enough brains—or too much brains, not enough beauty. Did she have the right balance?

He smiled again. A professional smile to the casual observer, but to Satin, it spelled promises and passion. It sent a signal to the electrodes in her heart. What she felt intrigued and frightened her.

She may have paid minimal attention when Randall was talking, but that wasn't the case when Drake presented his company's recommendations for possible marketing campaigns. She intently listened to his ideas, absorbing the comments made by the art director and copywriter.

"We'll leave these comps with you to give you a chance to review them," Drake said.

"We'll do just that," Randall said, rising from his seat. "I enjoyed meeting everyone and look forward to working with you," Satin said, making eye contact with the copywriter and art director. She turned her gaze to Drake—a lingering gaze—and then stood.

As the meeting ended, the art director and Randall engaged in conversation while walking to the lobby. The copywriter indicated that she would meet them in the reception area after stopping in the ladies' room. Satin intended to return to her office, but instead escorted Drake to the lobby.

"Congratulations on the new position," Drake said.

"Congratulations on winning the account."

"Thank you. We really wanted to win this account." Drake wanted to ask, "Can I take you to dinner?" but asked, "Where did you work before coming here?"

"For a company you've probably never heard of in Cleveland."

"Cleveland, Ohio?" Drake now understood why her name wasn't listed in the Atlanta's phone directory. It never occurred to him that she lived elsewhere.

"Not the one in Tennessee," she said with a mischievous grin.

"Welcome to Atlanta," he said, suppressing the desire to add, "May I show you around the city?" How inappropriate. How unprofessional. So he said, "I look forward to our next meeting."

Nine

Every family has a rock

Drake eyed the eight ball, studying its position in the middle of the red-velvet-topped pool table. He had a decision to make: whether to aim for the right- or left-corner pocket. Narrowing his eyes, he knelt down to pool table level, ascertaining the angle of his shot.

"Study long, study wrong," Damon teased.

"We're not playing cards. Pool requires a different type of skill."

"I don't think you have the skills to make that shot."

Drake ignored his brother's taunt and focused on the shot. "Fifty-fifty chance." He leaned over the table and positioned the pool stick between his middle fingers. "Right pocket."

Drake took the shot: The ball hit the right-corner pocket, and bounced out, rolling several inches away from its destination. "Damn!"

"Let me show you how a pro does it," bragged Damon. He successfully aimed for the two remaining low balls, before shooting the eight ball into the left-corner pocket. "In your face, baby." A wide grin spread across his broad face. On his head, he had a baseball cap with Atlanta Hawks on the front.

Drake raised a beer bottle to his lips. He took a

swig, draining its contents. "The night is young, not like you. Hitting thirty-three in two weeks."

"Not like you're far behind."

"I know," he said, arranging the balls inside the pool rack. "It doesn't bother me except that I thought I'd be married with a kid by now."

"Stop messing around with so many women, player, player." Damon playfully slapped Drake on the back.

"Everyone thinks I mess around with a lot of women. I'm certainly not sleeping with all the women I date. It's too dangerous."

"That's why you have to strap up."

"I'm careful," Drake said. "Remember the woman I told you about?"

"Yeah." Damon bent over the pool table. "Satin something." He aimed at the balls lined together in triangle formation, hitting and scattering them around the table.

"I found her, so to speak."

Damon chuckled. "You been hanging at the strip clubs."

"No, man, she's not a stripper. I told you I saw her at this new account. She was sitting in the lobby." With one shot, Drake dropped two balls into the corner pocket.

"A high-tech company."

"Would you believe she works for the company? I met her yesterday when I was there to present some marketing campaigns."

"Interesting coincidence."

"Interesting and funny. She thought I was interviewing for the position she got. She's the new product manager and I'm going to be working with her."

"That is funny," agreed Damon. "So now that you've met her, what are you going to do?"

"Take her out. I wanted to ask her yesterday, but it wasn't the right time."

"She's not married, is she?"

"I don't know." Drake rubbed his chin with his thumb. "I didn't notice a ring on her finger." His mouth turned down. "I hope not."

They finished another game of pool, and then sat down on opposite ends of the sofa. Damon grabbed the remote from the coffee table and scanned through the channels, stopping at ESPN.

"Lane told me you're worried about your job."

"I didn't want her to know." Damon cocked his head sideways. "Somehow I wasn't on the hit list. The rumor was that 20 percent of my department was going to be reduced, but the Grim Reaper bypassed us."

"Man, I know you're relieved."

They watched the second half of the basketball game, hooting and howling when a fight broke out between players.

"Something's going on with Alanna," Damon said during a commercial break.

"What do you mean?"

"She's been distant and real sensitive."

"Maybe she was worried about your job situation."

"I don't think that's it." Damon drew in a low breath, then let it out. "She won't let me touch her."

A heavy silence hung in the air. The conversation had taken an awkward turn into private marital territory, territory Drake preferred not to enter. "Have you asked her about it?"

"She's always tired or not in the mood," Damon said, exasperation heavy in his voice. "I'm starting to wonder if she's seeing somebody."

"I can't imagine Alanna doing that. She loves you, man, and the kids." In one sentence he could wipe away his brother's fear of betrayal. But he'd only be replacing it with a bigger fear, a fear that Alanna was trying to protect him from. "You two have one of the best marriages around. I know she's not messing around on you. Not Alanna. She's not like Glenda."

"I don't think she would," Damon said, scratching his head. "I'm just trying to figure out what's going on with her."

"You've had low points like this before."

"The last time she was pregnant." He laughed and said, "I'd be happy if she was pregnant."

"You want another kid?"

"There were three of us," Damon said, shrugging.

Drake nodded, wishing he had convinced Alanna to tell Damon, but she adamantly refused. She didn't want to reveal her doctor's suspicions until she knew with certainty, fervently praying that her doctor was wrong. Drake had agreed to escort Alanna to the hospital for testing.

"You know what your problem is?"

Drake gave his brother a puzzled stare. "What?"

"You think all women are like our mother."

"Your mother is here," the receptionist said to Drake upon entering his office.

"My mother?" Drake intoned, scowling his displeasure. He moaned aloud, realizing belatedly that Elle probably misunderstood his unhappy response. "I have such a busy day," he explained. "Are you sure?"

"Ms. Glenda Swanson."

"That's my mother," he said, wondering what brought her to midtown.

"She's so young," Elle gushed. "She looks like she could be your sister."

"She prides herself on looking young."

"I hope I look that good when I'm her age." Elle walked to the door. "I'll show her in."

Drake sent the E-mail he was working on when his mother strutted into his office dressed in a purple suede suit set that featured a zip-front jacket and short skirt. Knee-high boots and a purse complemented the outfit. She indeed looked young enough to be his sister. "Hello, Glenda."

"I know I should have called," Glenda squealed, abandoning her usual husky voice in her excitement, "but you would have told me that you're too busy." She flung her arms wide. "It's so rare that I get to see you working." She gave him a fierce hug. "You the boss man of this operation."

"Have a seat. Can I get you anything to drink?"

"I'm not in the mood for tea or Coca-Cola."

Drake nodded, and walked to the wet bar in the corner of his office. He opened a cabinet door and removed a bottle of whiskey. He dropped ice cubes in a glass and poured whiskey inside.

"I drink it straight, baby," Glenda said.

"I know." Drake poured a glass of Coke for himself, and then handed the glass of whiskey to Glenda before joining her on the couch.

"I hear you're planning a surprise party for Damon."

"I'm helping Alanna."

"Make sure you have plenty of food and liquor," she advised, removing a pack of cigarettes from her purse. "Mind if I smoke in here?"

Drake lifted his shoulders. "I'll get you an ashtray." He got up, located one, and returned to the couch. "Here you go."

"Thank you." Glenda flicked the flame from the lighter to the cigarette, inhaled until the end of the cigarette glowed. "I don't say it very often, but I am proud of you, son." She puffed on the cigarette, surveying his office, containing typical office décor: desk, two chairs, a conference table, and bookshelf. A large fish tank and unique artwork added personality to the room. "You haven't changed much since I was last here."

"That picture is new," he said, pointing to the large painting on the wall. "A client gave it to me when we did some work for him." Drake flicked his wrist to view his Cartier watch. "What's going on?"

She took a long drag on her cigarette. "I'm in trouble."

Knitting his brows together, Drake cocked his head sideways. "What kind of trouble?"

"Trouble with the law."

Drake widened his gray eyes as a creeping sensation crawled through his skin. "Have you been arrested?"

She inhaled her cigarette and blew out a billow of smoke. "That's what I'm afraid of."

Drake studied his mother's face, whose shape and color were so much like his. He was stunned, and waited anxiously for Glenda to explain. After a long silent pause, he impatiently asked, "Exactly what are you talking about?"

"This fellow I've been seeing . . . I think he's been up to no good."

"The one I met? Henry—"

"Not Henry!" Glenda flicked her hand in a dismissive gesture. "He's a regular old working Joe."

"Who are you talking about?"

"Arthur Davis."

"Who is he?"

"You've never met him. He has his own business, a telemarketing firm."

"Go on."

"He said he needed a manager and I told him I'd help out. I told him that I don't like working nine to five every day, but he was willing to be flexible with me." Finished with her cigarette, Glenda stamped it out in the ashtray. "After a while, I figured that he wasn't on the up and up. He sends out those letters to people that say you've won money."

"But you have to buy something to get the prize money," Drake said.

"They send in their credit card numbers to claim their prize. You'd be surprised how many people are suckers." Glenda clucked her tongue in disbelief. "I've seen some files and some things I don't think is cool. I think he's doing something shady with their credit cards."

Drake's features knotted into an expression of disgust. "Quit! Don't work for him anymore."

"That's the problem." Glenda blinked, her heavily mascaraed eyes fluttering in frustration. "He won't let me quit."

Drake frowned. "He can't make you work there. You never stay on a job for long anyhow."

Glenda drank some of her whiskey. "He threatened me."

"He what?" His tone was angry, indignant.

"He threatened me!" she repeated sharply, communicating the meaning of her words with the intensity of her gaze.

Drake rubbed his hands over his face. He swallowed to lubricate his throat. "Have you told anyone else?"

"Damon has his family to take care of and Derek is so . . . irresponsible." She removed another cigarette from the packet. "I figure the only person Arthur will listen to is you." Her hands trembled while lighting the cigarette. "I've known him a long time. He can be dangerous."

Drake stared at Glenda. The fear on her face was something he'd never seen before. It cut to the core of his love for her. She wasn't around very much when he was growing up. She wasn't mother Madonna. Despite the complexities of their relationship, he had to help her.

He just wasn't sure if he could.

Ten

Satin discovers another side of herself

The fancy skirt outfit featured a sheer button-front top and sequin trim around the blouse and skirt. The skirt was short—several inches above her knees—and the shirt was sheer, except for the sequin trim around her breasts. It was a bold, funky attention-getting outfit.

Satin was wearing it.

She donned the outfit, with Zandra's insistence, complete with sexy, three-inch slingbacks and a set of rhinestone hoops and bangles. She wouldn't have worn the ensemble in Cleveland. Upon entering the Peachtree Street nightclub she felt like Cinderella at the queen's ball, no longer hidden in the shadows of everyone's perceptions. She strutted through the club and didn't recognize anyone. It was an unusual experience. If she were at a club at home, she'd know most of the people there; and the ones she didn't directly know, probably knew someone she knew. Once frightened by anonymity, she felt strangely empowered by its obscurity.

The music changed from a slow ballad to an up-tempo dance song. The effect was immediate: Couples crowded the small dance floor.

Satin and Zandra sat at a table talking about the

party. Zandra knew one of the club owners and was frequently invited to the private parties held there. A tall, light-skinned man interrupted their conversation, inquiring whether or not Satin wanted to dance. The disc jockey was playing one of her favorite songs, so she agreed. Satin followed the man to a spot on the crowded dance floor. Usually self-conscious about dancing, Satin let the rhythm of the music invade her senses and released some of her inhibitions.

At the edge of the dance floor, Drake spotted Satin. He had expected to see her, but was nonetheless excited. He watched her laughing and dancing, and an unexpected feeling crept over him—a twinge of jealousy—even though his rational mind tried to disqualify the feeling.

From behind, Drake suddenly felt a firm tap on his shoulder. He turned around, coming face-to-face with the last person he wanted to see—Natasha Owens. She was tall, beautiful, and sexily attired. But she was also selfish, spoiled, and very cunning. She made it no secret that she wanted him, cockily declaring that he was going to fall in love with her. He'd taken her to dinner, and escorted her to several events. That's what she wanted most—an opportunity to be seen and maybe even signed by a record producer. She wanted to see more of him, but Drake wanted to see less of her. He'd learned to sever dating friendships early, before they became relationships with high expectations. But Natasha was unwilling to let Drake define the limitations of their friendship.

"Hey, lover," she said, taking both of Drake's hands in hers, and giving him the full impact of her fluttering green eyes. Sometimes her eyes were gray, sometimes blue, and sometimes hazel.

"Natasha," he said, releasing his hands from her grip. "How are you?"

"Lonely," she said in a little baby-girl voice.

"Somehow I don't believe that," he said, knowing her reputation around town.

"Dance with me?"

"No, thanks." His eyes darted to the dance floor, but Satin had disappeared from sight, swallowed up by a sea of dancing couples.

"Come on." Natasha tugged his hand. "Dance with me."

"Okay," he muttered. "One dance." He followed Natasha onto the dance floor, going deep into the crowd. Securing a spot, they started dancing. Within seconds, he realized that he was dancing next to Satin, who was now dancing with someone else.

Twisting and turning, moving and grooving to the heavy hip-hop beat, they ended up making eye contact. He smiled at her and she smiled back. No words were spoken, but much was said in the way they smiled at each other. When the song ended, Drake bid good night to Natasha, and then followed Satin off the dance floor, not noticing that Natasha was behind him. He was relieved when Satin departed from her dancing partner.

Satin returned to her table and was about to sit down when she heard someone call her name. She didn't immediately recognize the voice, but the beat of her heart accelerated. She turned around, not realizing that her heart knew the sound of his voice. "Hello, Drake," she said, giving him a casual smile.

"This is a nice surprise. How are you, Satin?"

"Great!"

"Having a good time?"

"Yes. Very much so," she said. "What about you?"

He nodded. "Griffin always throws hot parties."

"Oh, Drake, this is my good friend Zandra," she said, introducing them. "Zandra, this is Drake."

Zandra rose from the table and extended her hand. "Nice to meet you." She grinned at him. "I've seen you around town."

"Pleasure to meet you," he said, nodding. "How do you know Satin?"

"We went to college together," Zandra said. "Satin was the good little student and I was the wild one."

Satin laughed. "She talked me into wearing this wild outfit."

Desire glistening in his eyes, Drake allowed his gaze to roam her body. "It looks very good on you."

"This isn't my usual style, but I kind of like it."

"Introduce us," Natasha suddenly said.

Desire instantly disappeared from Drake's face as he turned to Natasha. "I didn't know you were standing there." Annoyance registered in his voice. He introduced the women to each other.

"Hello," Natasha said, hovering near Drake.

"Thanks for the dance, Natasha."

An awkward pause followed before Natasha acknowledged that Drake preferred the company of the women she'd just met. She glared at Satin and Zandra, and cast a disappointed glance in Drake's direction. "I'll see you later, " she said before walking away.

"I think she's mad," Satin said, unnerved by the sudden streak of jealousy.

"We didn't come here together," Drake explained.

"That doesn't mean you won't be leaving together," Zandra said with chortle of laughter.

Drake focused on Satin, desire returning to his eyes. "There's only one woman I'm interested in."

"I don't go home with men I don't know," Satin said.

"I think I'll leave you two to get to know each

other," Zandra said, rising from her seat, and then walking away.

"Do you mind?" Drake asked, his hands wrapped around the top of the chair.

"No."

"So what do you think of Atlanta so far?" he inquired while sitting down.

"I love it. I'm new here, so my perspective is fresh, off-the-boat excitement, but I'm feeling this place. How long have you lived here?"

"All my life. I grew up in Southwest Atlanta."

"Is Ashby Street over that way?"

"Yes."

"My great-aunt lives over there."

His brother's question about her marital status popped in his mind. Drake surveyed her hands for an engagement or wedding ring. Her hands were long and delicate, and there wasn't a diamond ring on either hand. "Did you come here by yourself?" he asked, wondering if she liked to hold hands and realizing how much he missed the smallest tokens of affection that a relationship can bring.

"All by my little self," she joked.

"That's a courageous move." He paused to clear his throat. "Did you leave a boyfriend in Cleveland?"

Satin shook her head. "I—"

"Excuse me, Drake," said a pretty young woman, interrupting their conversation.

"Hello, Mari," he said. "How are you?"

"I'm fine. I'm working for a new company, Comm Services. I'm the director of marketing communications."

"Congratulations."

"We're revamping all our collateral and may be looking for an agency to do some work for us." Mari handed Drake her business card. "Right now we're getting the budget approved, but I would love to work with you again."

"Great. When you get budget approval—"

"I'll definitely be in touch," she said with a seductive smile. "Maybe even before then."

As Mari walked away, Drake said, "Sorry about that. She worked for a client. So, where were we? You left your boyfriend in Cleveland—"

"No, I don't believe in loose ends. We're not together."

Drake couldn't stop the smile that spread across his face.

She couldn't stop herself from responding, "Why are you smiling like that?"

"You're not married," he said, touching her hands. "And you don't have a boyfriend. That means I can ask you a question."

"What?" she asked with a curious expression.

"Would you go out to dinner with me?"

His question was as unexpected as the butterflies nesting in her stomach. "I'm flattered, but I don't think it would be a very good idea."

"Why?"

"Three reasons."

He stretched his eyebrows. "Three?"

"I don't go out with men who are in a relationship."

"I'm not in a relationship."

"What about Natasha?"

Drake lifted his shoulders. "I'm not involved with her or anyone else," he explained in a matter-of-fact tone, his gaze unflinching. "What's reason number two?"

"We're going to be working together."

"We don't work for the same companies. I can maintain my professional objectivity." He leaned closer to her. "Can you?" he challengingly asked.

"Yes," she said simply.

"What's reason number three?"

Satin shook her head. She didn't want to tell him her third reason: *Your very presence makes my heart race. You make me feel out of sync with time and place. Something mysterious happens inside whenever I see your face.* And she didn't want to lie. "I can't tell you reason number three."

"Why?"

"I just can't."

"Okay," he said, his face reflecting disappointment. "I have another question for you. How do you explain the fact that we see each other in the lobby and then meet again in the same place months later?"

"I don't know," she answered, but wondered the very same thing. Was it Divine Providence or pure co-incidence? She chose the latter. "Pure coincidence."

"Or could it be your reason number three? The one you won't divulge."

She gave him a sharp look. Yes, she was resisting him because of the way he made her feel, and per-haps there was a connection between her feelings today and her feelings from their first meeting, feel-ings that were opening unknown places in her heart.

"But if there's no connection then we probably won't just run into each other again and reason num-ber three will disappear." He rose from the table. Before leaving, he kissed her hand. "Good night."

In Zandra's car, a couple hours later, Satin kicked off her shoes and complained about her aching feet.

"I don't want to hear about your feet," Zandra said, turning the steering wheel as she rounded a corner. "I want to know when you're going out with Drake."

"I'm not." Satin adjusted the passenger seat to a supine position.

"He didn't ask you out? He had that look in his eyes."

"What look?"

Zandra flicked her eyes at Satin. "That I-want-her look."

"Did he really look at me like that?"

Zandra made a hissing sound with her mouth. "You're not blind, are you?"

"No. I just tried to convince myself that I was imagining things."

"Don't go into denial land," Zandra said. "Did he ask you out?"

"Yes, but I turned him down."

"Why?"

Should she lie to her friend or admit the truth? "He scares me," Satin confessed.

"Girl, get out of wimpy land," Zandra admonished. "Besides, my mama used to tell me, 'You can't run from your heart.'"

"You told the committee that all the legal matters have been resolved," Richard Creighton said to Jacob Murphy. The cigar between his teeth churned up clouds of smoke that gradually dissipated into a low blue haze hovering overhead. With his eyes narrowed appraisingly, he said accusingly, "But you lied."

Jacob took a deep breath, inflated his cheeks, then slowly exhaled. The man standing beside him was bigger, taller, and older than he was. But more importantly, Richard Creighton was more powerful and influential. The man was smart and deceptive. And Jacob realized that only the truth would save him. "We've run into a snag."

"Explain," Richard said in a demeaning tone.

"The land isn't free and clear. A title search revealed that it's part of a will that's been contested."

"Continue."

"Susan Mitchell willed some of her land to her maid. The maid died and bequeathed the land to female relatives. The executors of the estate want to sell the land, so they offered to pay the maid's relatives money in exchange for them signing papers that would relinquish their claim to the land," Jacob explained. "But one of the relatives apparently refuses to sign the papers and they can't do anything until everyone agrees."

Richard thrust his head forward, resembling a ferocious pit bull. "You do understand this conversation is completely off the record." Richard had anticipated the direction of their conversation, which was the reason they were meeting in an abandoned baseball field.

"Understood," Jacob murmured.

"There are ways around this obstacle. Getting paperwork through county records shouldn't be difficult. Eventually you'll need proper documentation, but in the meantime, get the title clerk to work some magic. You can get a temporary order."

"But it can be appealed," Jacob said, preferring to follow proper procedures.

"Worry about it when it's appealed. Right now we need to break ground and show some progress. I have several deals in the works that are dependent on that shopping center going up." Cigar in the corner of his mouth, Richard churned up even greater clouds of smoke. "Some expensive subdivisions and businesses have expressed interest in nearby sites. Imagine the impact on the property value. It's a gold mine and you don't let one simple signature keep you away from the gold."

"The committee seemed concerned about the architectural rendering, so I've commissioned a new rendering."

"Look, I know all the stall games. Tell that crap to the media. But I want you to listen and understand what I'm telling you." He raised his eyes and pointedly met Jacob's gaze. "I want it done."

"I understand."

"Understand this: I'm the committee." Richard's eyes flashed like multiple razor blades.

Jacob's patrician features expressed a look of disbelief. "I know you're the major stakeholder, but—"

"I'm the committee."

Understanding filled Jacob's face. "You're the financial source for—"

"Let's not name names. I want this problem taken care of ASAP! I have some major investors on the hook and I have no intention of letting them go."

"Understood."

The meeting over, Jacob headed to his car. It was a beautiful, cloudless day, but Jacob didn't notice. He was too worried about the cloud hanging over his head. Getting into his silver BMW, Jacob turned on the ignition and raced out of the park, heading to his office in Buckhead.

Jacob had to arrange his day to accommodate the top priority on his to-do list. Contacting the maid's relative who wouldn't sign the paperwork was now priority one.

Eleven

Growing up without your mother

The first view of his father's house always had the same effect—a rush of childhood memories. Depending on Drake's mood, the memories would replay like a movie on fast forward: undecipherable images, illogical sequences, and disjointed actions. Sometimes he paused to fully retrieve a memory that he savored, such as his father playing baseball with them in the backyard, or the moments spent together repairing cars and motorcycles. Other memories—the unexpected, emotional visits from his usually missing-in-action mother—he let fast forward to the archived recesses of his memories. The memories didn't play while driving along the highway to Riverdale, near Hartsfield International Airport. Nor did they begin when he exited the highway or neared the street. The memories reappeared—oftentimes uninvited—when he pulled up in front of his father's house.

Drake parked his car, walked up the small path, and started up the steps. He heard the television playing loudly in the living room and imagined his father napping in his favorite recliner chair. So he simultaneously banged on the door and pressed the doorbell.

A tall, thin, chocolate-skinned man with gray hair and broad features swung the door open. Roosevelt Swanson's mouth fell open, accentuating the full features. "Drake! Why didn't you tell me you were coming?"

"Hey, Pops." Drake embraced the older man who was just an inch or two below his six-foot-two height. "You know I stop by on your off days."

"You and Derek." Roosevelt gave his son a welcoming smile. "Except when Derek pops in, he usually needs money. He was here two days ago."

Drake shook his head. "I don't want to know about it." His younger brother was fun loving, charming, and irresponsible; he had a tendency to get into financial trouble. Drake had bailed him out on numerous occasions—paid his rent, electric, and phone bills, and loaned him down payment money for a car. He'd even helped him find jobs, but Derek never stayed with an employer for long. Hence, he perpetuated his own financial difficulties and Drake refused to support his brother's self-destructive behavior.

Drake followed his father into the living room, where he observed the usually messy room was rather tidy. "Looks like a maid's been here," he said. The newspaper was neatly stacked on the table, the ashtrays cleaned, the furniture dusted, the floor freshly vacuumed.

"I'm expecting company."

Drake sniffed the air. He recognized the scent—it was Old Spice cologne. He then noticed his father's attire: a suit and polished shoes. "You're looking rather . . . debonair. Where are you going?"

"On a date."

"Oh, yeah," Drake said, dropping his large frame onto the sofa, trying to recall memories of his father with another woman. There was a pretty young woman from down the street who used to regularly visit his father, and there was the mysterious Ms. Victoria who called on the telephone, but was never seen by the boys. Over the years, he concluded that his father had lady friends, but none of them could replace Glenda in his heart. "Who with?"

"Velda Mae Robinson. She goes to the church," the older man said, sitting down in his easy chair, smiling fondly. "She's a good-looking woman. She's God-fearing and keeps active with the church."

Drake noticed the gleam in his father's eyes. "You really like this woman, don't you?"

Roosevelt smiled. "I've taken a real fancy to her. She warms my heart and she can cook. She's bringing dinner over."

Drake chuckled. "Does she have kids? Where does she live? Does she work?"

"She lives nearby. She's a widow. Her husband died about ten years ago. She's got four grown kids. Two live in other cities and two live here. Now what was your other question?"

"Does she work?"

"She works for an insurance company. Been there for over twenty years."

"I'm glad you found someone you enjoy being with."

"It's about time, huh?" Roosevelt remarked, laughing. "You need to find you somebody, too."

Drake nodded, and then said, "Pops, I came by to see if you want to look at motorcycles with me. I've been thinking about buying a new one."

"I can't go with you today, son. Velda Mae going to be here real soon. She makes the best liver and onions you ever tasted. It just melts in your mouth."

From the look in his father's eyes, Drake surmised that Velda Mae's talents extended beyond the kitchen and into the bedroom.

The doorbell rang, bringing Roosevelt immediately

to his feet. "That's her now." Roosevelt glanced in the mirror and patted his hair. "I need a haircut, but do I look all right?"

"Pops, you look handsome and suave—"

"Suave." Roosevelt chuckled. "I like that."

A few minutes later, after stopping in the kitchen to drop off several platters of food, Roosevelt returned to the living room accompanied by Velda Mae Robinson. The attractive, middle-aged woman greeted Drake with a warm, friendly smile. "I've heard so much about you. It's good to finally meet you."

Rising from the sofa, Drake found himself unexpectedly hugged by the woman. Stepping back, he said, "It's a pleasure meeting you."

"You're the one with gray eyes. The beautiful gray eyes," Velda Mae said.

"Thank you," Drake said, hoping the woman wouldn't inquire where he inherited his eyes. Both sides of the family claimed a relative who had gray eyes, but Drake had never seen a picture of anyone. He was never comfortable with the subject. It reminded him of family whisperings about his paternity.

"You're so handsome, too. I can't believe you're not married," she said.

"I'd like to get married," Drake admitted. "I just haven't found the right woman."

"Oh, you will," she confidently said. "God may have already sent her to you, but you just don't know it yet."

"Or maybe she doesn't know it yet," he remarked, wondering if her comment was conversational chatter or an uncanny prediction. Either way, only one woman came to mind: Satin Holiday.

"Are you going to have dinner with us?" Velda Mae asked.

"No, ma'am. I'm going to head back to the office. I have some work to do."

"I like hearing a young black man talk about work. It's good for your soul."

"Yes, ma'am," Drake said.

"I'm going into the kitchen to fix up your father's dinner," Velda Mae said. "I don't believe in the microwave, so I have to heat up the stove."

"Enjoy your dinner. And I hope to see you again."

"You will," she said confidently. "You will." Velda Mae exited the living room to go into the kitchen in the back of the house.

"I like her, Pops." He swatted his father's shoulders. "She seems mighty confident that she's going to be around."

Roosevelt scratched the top of his head. "That's 'cause we've been talking about marriage."

"Pops! Are you serious?"

"Serious as a heart attack," he said, patting Drake on the back. "And I'm not about to have one."

"Congratulations! I'm glad you found someone special."

"Me, too," Roosevelt said. "I've been lonely for a long time. And the funny thing is I was so used to it that I forgot I was lonely." He probed his son's face. "You know what I mean?"

"I understand," Drake said. His father's words were an echo of his feelings. They were from two different generations, yet both felt the same sense of loneliness. Drake submerged his loneliness by surrounding himself with work and fulfilling his playboy image, but his heart longed for something more. The realization of that desire was triggered when he saw Satin. Somehow she reminded him of what was missing in his life. Was she the person to fill the void or was she just the person to remind him of the void?

"Don't spend your life wishing for something that can't be."

"Like you did with Glenda?" Drake posed, venturing into a subject they rarely discussed. His father's response was a slight shrug and a remorseful frown. "I'm not waiting for Tavia to come back."

"Good," Roosevelt said, smiling. "Any prospects?"

"I have met someone. I can't stop thinking about her."

"What are you doing about it?"

"I asked her out, but she turned me down. I guess I have to ask again."

"Sometimes a woman needs a little prodding to open up." Rubbing his chin, Roosevelt chuckled. "I don't mean *that* kind of prodding."

Standing in the hall, Drake laughed. "I get your meaning. Why don't you bring Ms. Velda Mae to Damon's birthday party? Introduce her to the family."

"I think I will," Roosevelt said, a thoughtful smile on his face. "I think I will."

When the door opened, everyone in the hospital waiting room would look to see if the woman opening the door was the one they'd accompanied to the testing center. The women who came through the door were tall and short, attractive and unattractive, skinny and fat. They were a diverse group, widely ranging in race, age, and socioeconomic stratosphere. All so very different, yet the expressions on their faces were frighteningly similar—worry and fear.

Drake had brought his laptop to do some work while waiting for Alanna to be tested. He'd fired up the computer and began reviewing some files. But the opening and closing of doors, one marked Enter and the other marked Exit, was distracting. In the life-and-death atmosphere of gloom and doom, he was unable to concentrate.

Realizing the futility of his efforts, he powered off the computer and returned it to the case. Like many others in the room, he scanned through some waiting room magazines and listlessly watched one of the popular judge shows playing on the television in the room.

He was worried about Alanna and the impact positive results would have on his brother. Damon would be devastated, his niece's and nephew's lives shattered. He could certainly relate to the empty feeling of growing up motherless. No, his mother hadn't died, but she was rarely around. In his mind, he was a motherless child. He adjusted—it was the way of his childhood. He certainly wasn't the only motherless boy in the neighborhood. His mother wasn't an addict or anything embarrassing like a prostitute. Glenda simply didn't want to be a mother. She wanted to be a famous singer, but became a lounge club singer. The selfishness of her decision always nagged at him, leaving his heart empty where a mother's love should be. He didn't want Lane and D.J.—Damon Jr.—to feel that same kind of emptiness.

Flipping through a magazine, he found himself thinking about Satin. How much she stayed on his mind. How much he wanted to get to know her. How often her name replayed in his life. Reflecting on the uncertainty of life, he decided that he couldn't let another tomorrow pass without contacting her. Fate had intervened, moving the mysterious forces of life to lead her to Atlanta. Fate had interceded, making sure they encountered each other—at work and a party. If fate didn't strike again, he would have to take fate by the hand.

The door opened and everyone turned to see who was there. Alanna slowly entered the waiting room, a slight smile edging the corners of her lips as she valiantly tried to hide her fear.

"Are you okay?" Drake asked.

"I'm fine," she claimed.

"Do you need to sit down and rest before leaving? Do you want a glass of water or something to eat?"

Alanna shook her head. "I just want to get out of here," she whispered in anguish.

"Let's go."

No words were exchanged when they walked out of the hospital, nor did they talk in the car while following the exit signs down the parking lot ramp to the highway. They were silent until the hospital was several exits away, broken by Alanna's loud, weary sigh.

"It's gonna be all right," Drake said, squeezing her hand.

"I've been praying and I believe God answers prayers."

"Yes, he does," Drake affirmed.

Tears welling in her eyes, her voice cracked. "I can't leave my babies."

"You won't, Alanna. We have to think positive."

She nodded. "Damon knows something's wrong. Has he asked you?"

"Yes, but I didn't tell him anything."

"I think he thinks I'm having an affair."

"He mentioned that. I told him it's ridiculous. He doesn't really think you are, he just knows something's wrong and he's searching for some kind of explanation."

"Are you going to advise me to have sex with him and—"

"We didn't get that deep."

"I know how close you are. That's why I really appreciate you keeping this to yourself."

"Have you told anyone else?" Drake inquired. "Your mother or your sister?"

"No, I didn't want to worry them."

"You're not going back to work, are you?"

"No. I took the day off. I'm going to take a nap until the kids get out of school." Alanna said. "Did you ever go out with that woman you met?"

Drake gave her a curious look.

"Damon told me," she explained. "He was excited that you met someone you like."

"I haven't gone out with her."

"Oh, there's something I been meaning to tell you about Tavia."

A tight expression formed on his face. "What about her?"

"She's going to be in town to shoot her next film."

"And Monet Cosmetics has selected her to be their spokesperson," he said, while turning into Alanna's subdivision.

"How do you know?" Alanna asked.

"We might develop her campaign for Monet Cosmetics. We bid on the project last month."

"Are you going to be comfortable working with her?" she asked in a concern-filled voice, remembering the devastation on his face when she informed him that Tavia was not going to walk down the aisle to marry him.

"We haven't won the account yet. And if we do, business is business."

"I just don't want her to break your heart again," Alanna said.

"She won't," he said, pulling into her driveway. "Get some rest. I'll check on you later."

Twelve

The velocity of curiosity

Jacob Murphy didn't believe in wasting time. Nor did he like waiting, waiting on someone else's decision before he could do what he needed. But he was in no position to protest or proceed.

He had little choice but to wait for Satin Holiday's arrival. Or more importantly, for her signature. He flipped his wrist to check his watch. She wasn't late—he was just anxious, anxious to move forward with the project, anxious to get the creditors off his back and anxious to placate Richard Creighton. Their last meeting surprised him. More to the point, the man's unveiled threat shocked Jacob. He'd heard that Richard could be prickly and dangerous. He'd been pricked and didn't want to be probed.

As he sipped some water, he noticed an attractive black woman enter the restaurant. She was stunning. And when he realized that the hostess was bringing her to his table, he comforted himself with the possibility that beauty might be the woman's only talent. Influencing her to sign the paperwork might be easy.

Jacob stood when she arrived at the table, and introduced himself. "I'm so glad you could join me for lunch."

"You were quite insistent," she said, sitting opposite him. "Besides, I thought this would give me a chance to experience one of Atlanta's finest restaurants."

They chatted about Atlanta, sharing childhood experiences about visits and their decisions to move to Atlanta. Jacob revealed that he came to Atlanta to attend Georgia Tech, and planned to return to his hometown after graduation, but stayed to accept a job with a local company. He was surprised when Satin divulged her professional background and interest in becoming a lawyer.

The waiter arrived with their lunch and then Jacob broached the reason for their meeting. "I understand that you and other relatives have inherited some valuable property from your great-aunt. But you don't want to sell the land."

"That's correct," she said.

"Everyone else wants to sell the land. But you don't. If you don't mind my asking, why?"

Satin lifted her shoulders. "I just want to keep the land. I like the idea of owning property."

"But you have no idea what's at stake."

"What's that?"

"A shopping center. The development of a community. Even the expansion of metro Atlanta."

She shook her head. "I don't know anything about all that. I don't know that it really concerns me."

"What concerns me is building that shopping center," Jacob said. "At this juncture, we can't move forward." He sipped some water. "I'd like to offer you an incentive to sign the estate's paperwork."

"What kind of incentive?"

"In addition to the money you'll get from the Mitchell estate, I'll pay you a signing bonus fee."

"How much?"

"The amount has to be negotiated. At minimum, $5,000. But you have to act quickly."

"This is all legal?" Satin questioned.

"It's like a signing bonus. My attorney would draw up the paperwork. It would be a confidential agreement."

"I couldn't tell my family about it?"

"The offer wouldn't be extended to others. The offer is contingent upon your agreement to sign the papers immediately."

"In other words, I won't get the 'bonus' until I've signed the papers."

Satin studied Jacob's face. He appeared to be respectable, but she was uncertain about his trustworthiness and even more uncomfortable with his proposed arrangement. "I have to think about it."

"The offer's only good for twenty-four hours and the agreement would be confidential." Jacob gave Satin a serious look. "Highly confidential."

"I'd have to have an attorney look over the paperwork before I sign anything," Satin said.

"Of course," Jacob said.

"This is going to be the wildest club you've ever been to," Zandra said, stopping her black Lexus in front of Club Caribbean for valet parking. "People get out of control in here."

Satin's hand rested on the door handle. "If it's that wild I don't want to go in."

"It's not the weekend, so it shouldn't be too crazy," Zandra said.

"This isn't the place where you see people kissing— men kissing men, and women kissing women?"

"Girl, I wouldn't take you to a place like that." Zandra handed her keys to the valet attendant and got out of the car. "It's a cool club. It's kind of like an all-in-one vacation resort for club hoppers."

Club Caribbean offered more than a dance floor, banging beats, flashing lights, and an overpriced bar. Club Caribbean was a multitude of party rooms with dance floors interconnected by a state-of-the-art sound system and powerful speakers. Each room had its own theme and entertainment activities, ranging from virtual reality games to cosmic bowling. On Friday and Saturday nights, the same music played in every room for several hours.

Inside the club, Satin and Zandra searched for the Aruba Room; each party room was named after an island in the Caribbean. "Is that Da Spoiled?" Satin asked, referring to the multiplatinum selling female rapper who lived in Atlanta. The braided, jewelry-adorned rapper was hunched over a pool table.

Zandra stopped to peek inside the Jamaica Room. "That's her."

"And is that Little—"

"Yes. Now don't go running over to them acting all starstruck."

"Zandra, you know me better than that," Satin said with a slightly offended look.

"Sometimes people see celebrities and lose their mind."

Taking the escalator to the upper level, Satin said, "I just want to know how you get into places like this. With celebrities walking around."

"I told you I'm in the mix. You didn't believe me, huh?" Zandra playfully swatted Satin on the arm. "I got a lot of connections from my writing gig with *Jezebel* magazine."

"How do you know about the video shoot?"

"What can I say? I'm in the know." Zandra pointed to the sign that read Aruba Room.

They swept into the room as a classic Temptations song began to play. Considering the average age of the crowd was probably twenty-one, Satin wondered if they ever heard the song, except through a sample on a rap song. "Why the old music?" Satin asked.

"The theme of the video is from the sixties and seventies. The rapper goes back in time. He raps the song to the audience who never, of course, heard of rap music," Zandra explained. "They boo him off the stage and he returns to his time and takes some of the people with him."

"It sounds very interesting. How do you know all this?"

"I told you, I'm in—"

"The know," Satin said, laughing with her.

They found an empty table in the open area of the club. Satin sat down, but Zandra remained standing.

"You're not going to be upset if I mingle a bit?" Zandra asked.

"Oh, please, don't leave me. I don't know anybody here." Seeing the serious expression on Zandra's face, Satin said, "I was joking."

"I remember when you'd get upset if I didn't stay with you in a club."

"I'm all growed up," Satin teased in a babylike voice.

"I'll come back and introduce you around, but first I've got some business to take care of."

"I'll be fine. I'll sit here, enjoy the music, and celebrity gaze."

"Oh, there is someone you know here. The fine brother with the smile you can't forget." Zandra bent down to whisper in her ear. "The one that scares you."

"Drake is here? You knew he was going to be here?"

"I assumed he might be here," Zandra answered, raising her thinly arched brows. "His company does a lot of work for So Cool Records. By the way, his table is right there." She pointed at the table in the nearby corner.

Satin wished he were much farther away. What would he think of her skimpy black dress? "Why didn't you tell me?"

"Because you would have stayed home. Daah!"

"Bye! Go! Leave!" Satin said, making shooing motions with her hands. "We'll catch up later."

"Later," Zandra said, and then walked into the crowd.

Satin observed Drake's table. There were two very attractive women sitting with him. She watched him get up from the table, the women seemingly reluctant for their conversation to end. Upon seeing her, Drake smiled and waved, indicating that he wanted to speak with her.

She waited for him to come to her table. Gladys Knight's song "If I Were Your Woman" began to play as she scooped a glass of wine from a passing waiter's tray. Two other women approached Drake as he made his way toward her. He spoke with them briefly and stepped toward her table. She noticed one of the women slip something in his jacket pocket. Was it a business card or a condom? She felt a rush of jealousy, confused by its irrational intensity.

"Satin," he said, when he finally reached her. "I'm glad you waited."

"I was admiring your fan club." She sipped her wine. "Impressive."

"It's not what you think."

Satin cocked her head back. "If I were your woman, you wouldn't want another woman," she proclaimed. She didn't sing along with the song, but spoke the words with confidence and conviction. Satin wondered if she was merely repeating the song's hook or was she speaking from the mysterious voice within

that claimed to know that there was a connection between them.

Joining her at the table, he said, "Is that so?"

"You'd be weak as a lamb, you couldn't walk away
from me," she said, grinning wickedly.

"Are you enjoying the song or are you trying to tell
me something?"

"Perhaps a little of both."

"Let's flip the script. If I were your man, you
wouldn't think about another man."

"Maybe I would," she said, then sipped her wine.
"Maybe I wouldn't."

"How are we going to find out if you won't go out
with me?"

She shrugged. "Another one of life's mysteries."

"This doesn't have to be a mystery. Or are you
afraid to find out what the mystery will reveal?"

Deadly afraid, she thought, but wouldn't say. She
was as curious as she was terrified. But at the moment,
curiosity was the more powerful emotion. What was it
about him that made her heart palpitate faster and
faster?

"Go out to dinner with me," he smoothly said. "We
can go out Friday or Saturday, whichever is more con-
venient for you."

Satin stared at him and then a grin slowly spread
across her face. "Right now," she impulsively said.
"How about right now?"

Satin had planned to spend a quiet evening at
home, curled up on the sofa with a book. She'd
started reading *Hidden Memories* by Robin Allen and
couldn't wait to find out why Sage hated her stepfa-
ther. But Zandra changed those plans and Satin
ended up at Club Caribbean where her plans for the

evening changed again. She hadn't planned to have dinner with Drake Swanson or go on a horse-and-buggy tour of downtown Atlanta.

"As many times as I've been here, I've never done this," she said, huddled next to Drake in the horse-drawn carriage.

"How often did you come here?"

"Almost every summer. My dad works at a Ford plant and he'd take off from work to drive down to Atlanta to visit his relatives. One of his brothers used to live here."

"My father works at a Ford plant, too. He works on the floor building cars."

"My father does the same thing," she said, laughing.

"I like your mole," he said, touching the mole with his finger.

"My mole?" She giggled. "Kids used to tease me about my Marilyn Monroe mole."

"And I like your hands." He caressed her hands, and then brought one to his mouth, kissing the back of her hand.

When the carriage ride ended, Satin checked her watch. It was later than she thought. "Zandra! I forgot to tell her I was leaving." Panic was in her voice. "And I don't have my cell phone with me."

"Use mine," Drake offered, removing the cell phone from his pocket and placing it in her hand. "Please let me take you home."

Satin nodded, touched by the tenderness in his request. She dialed Zandra's number.

"Are you with Drake?" Zandra asked.

"How do you know?"

"Caller ID, silly," she answered. "But I knew anyway. A friend told me that you left with Drake."

"I thought you were worried."

"Nope," Zandra said. "So you need a ride or you're not coming home?"

"I'm coming home," she said, and then pressed the end button.

"You don't have to go home," he said, desire glistening as his eyes roamed her body, lingering on her breasts and thighs.

"I want to," she pointedly said.

Drake pulled into Satin's apartment complex. In a very gentlemanly fashion, he opened the passenger side door for Satin and then walked her up the stairs to the front door.

"This wasn't the evening I expected. I was going to stay home and read."

"It wasn't what I planned, but it was certainly better than I expected." He reached for the keys in her hand. "Allow me."

Before opening her apartment door, he opened the doorway to her heart with a kiss. Satin's plans for the evening definitely hadn't included the most dynamic kiss she'd ever experienced.

Thirteen

A gangster and a famous actress

All eyes were on Satin, standing in front of the whiteboard, looking professional and polished, even though she'd only had a few hours' sleep. Her boss, Randall, two employees from product development, and several associates from Marketing Missions listened as she outlined her plans and strategies for the product launch and identified the marketing campaign she'd chosen.

But Drake wasn't listening. His thoughts were elsewhere—where their lips had touched, where a kiss became kisses, intimate, passionate kisses, leading to the crossing of a boundary. A boundary as nebulous and undefined as the galaxy of the universe.

It was more than a kiss. He'd felt it and so had she. He'd seen it in her face when her eyes had opened— inviting him in, daring him to partake of more. And he had.

But now he wanted more than a kiss.

Drake suddenly realized that the center of attention had shifted from Satin to him. Everyone around the conference room table was looking at him, waiting for his response to a question he hadn't heard.

He cleared his throat. "Please repeat the question. I want to make sure I address all your concerns."

"Because we're changing our product release date, we need to move quickly to execute the marketing campaign," Satin explained in a neutral tone, suspecting he'd been distracted by thoughts of their kiss. "Can your company flex to the milestones?"

"Let me assure you that we are quick-change artists. We pride ourselves on being adaptable and flexible to meet our clients' needs." Drake exchanged confirming glances with the art director and copywriter. "We, of course, will do the same for you."

"That's what we want to hear," Randall said.

"To be clear, you don't want a new or different campaign," Drake probed. "You are basically moving up the schedule."

"Precisely," Randall said.

"We've added some features, so there may be some copy changes, but the overall look and feel of the Dr. Seuss campaign is compatible with the spirit of the product," Satin explained.

"Is there a particular reason for the schedule change?" Drake asked. "Are you trying to sync up the launch with a trade show or other communications vehicle?"

"Actually, Satin discovered a common link in the code that is a shortcut for some of the work that product development had anticipated," Randall said, smiling proudly at Satin as a parent would smile at their child.

"That's excellent," Drake said, making direct eye contact with Satin. "Congratulations, Satin." Although an admiring, appreciative smile was on his face, Satin's intelligence wasn't on his mind. Her lips and breasts, and buttocks and thighs were tickling his imagination. Lest his face betray his thoughts, Drake shifted his attention from Satin to her boss. "I'm sure you're excited about the new direction."

"Indeed we are," Randall said.

As the meeting came to a close, Drake found himself the focus of Satin's gaze. They shared a quiet communiqué. No words were spoken, no body movements, no interpretive gestures. Just eye-to-eye contact. In that second of communication, another boundary was crossed.

"Roberta is pregnant."

"Creative Inc. outbid us for the TechFactor account. I heard that we were $100,000 higher."

"Did you know that Sam is getting a divorce?"

"I heard that some big agency in New York is going to buy us."

"Ooh, Gregory is gay."

Gossip and speculation was being voiced by Marketing Missions employees convened in the large conference room while waiting for Drake. In between bites of Buffalo wings, meatballs, cheese, and nachos, rumor became fact and gossip sounded like the truth.

Speculation that the meeting was convened to announce bad news disappeared as soon as Drake arrived. His smile was too brilliant to be the bearer of bad news. By the time he walked to the front of the room, the contagion of his smile had spread.

Facing the employees of Marketing Missions, he said, "From the smiles on your faces, you must know I have some good news to share."

"We can't help it—you're so transparent," Brent teased.

Laughter sounded around the room.

"What I'm about to announce is something to be transparent about." He paused until everyone grew still in anticipation. "We've been selected by Monet Cosmetics to create an ad campaign for their newest spokesperson, actress Tavia Beaudeaux, who will—"

His announcement was interrupted by cheers and applause, high-fives and back slaps. Several minutes passed before he could continue. "This is a big feather in our caps, and elevates us with our existing clients. I can't stress how important it will be for us to perform beyond expectation. If they're happy with us, it can lead to additional projects with Monet Cosmetics and other Fortune 500 companies.

"I want to acknowledge the Devlon team," continued Drake. "They put together an excellent presentation." He acknowledged the efforts of each team member, highlighting their contributions to the project.

"I'm very excited about this opportunity and hope you share my enthusiasm. Together we can make it happen, " Drake said, concluding his good news announcement. He mingled with his staff, enjoying the catered lunch for the special occasion.

In the midst of the excitement, his thoughts turned to Satin. If he didn't have a date with Satin that evening, he would work late, crunching numbers for the Monet project. But work would have to wait. Spending time with Satin was a priority—albeit a personal one. It would be their third date and he wanted to do much more than kiss her. Hot, passionate, steamy kisses was all she would allow, as if she were afraid where kissing would lead. It would lead them to a place where boundaries didn't exist.

Returning his concentration to his work, Drake scheduled two meetings with employees before departing the room. His departure didn't end the gossip and speculation. Instead of whispering about various personal and business matters, there was one topic of conversation—Drake's relationship with the very famous Tavia Beaudeaux.

"I heard she left him standing at the altar."

"She chose an audition over him. You know that had to hurt."

"That audition landed her the role that made her a movie star."

"It will be interesting to see if sparks fly between them."

"Maybe she told Monet to pick us for the campaign cause maybe she left her heart in Atlanta."

"She dates the finest men in Hollywood."

"Yeah, but she ain't married anyone yet."

"And neither has he."

From outward appearances, Dream Enterprises appeared to be a legitimate business. In an older office park development, it was housed near respectable businesses: a doctor's office, a training development company, an eatery, and a real estate office.

Drake opened the door to Dream Enterprises and was greeted by the sound of incessantly ringing telephones and loudly played music.

A telephone pressed to her ear, the receptionist held out her finger and mouthed, "One minute." Drake sat on the couch, noticing the contrasting display of magazines. Black magazines, such as *Ebony, Jet* and *Essence*, were neatly piled on a table in front of the sofa. On the other side of the room, *Time, People, Redbook, Glamour,* and *Entertainment Weekly* were stacked on a small table between two chairs.

Drake didn't have a chance to decide which magazine to read when the receptionist spoke his name.

"I know you're Drake Swanson," she said, emphasizing his name. "Your mama has bragged all about you." The young, brazen woman leaned against her chair and surveyed Drake from head to toe. "She wasn't lying when she said you were her handsome son."

Drake nodded, observing that the receptionist's outfit would be inappropriate in most business environments. She wore skintight pants and a blouse that revealed huge breasts. Large gold hoops hung from her ears. Her fingernails were bright red and matched the mass of long braids.

"Mr. Arthur is ready to see you," she said. "I'll take you to his office, but if you want something to drink we can stop in the break room."

Drake declined her hospitable offer.

"We have plenty to drink. Visitors get to drink on the house but us hardworking employees got to pay," she explained. "Are you sure you don't want anything?"

"I'm sure."

"If you want something on the low-low, I can get you some rum or Hennessy or some Jack D."

"No," he repeated firmly.

"Your mama don't hesitate about getting her drink on, that's for sure."

"My mother has been grown for a long time."

"You're funny." The receptionist laughed, revealing several gold teeth. "Where your mama been? She ain't been to work in a couple of weeks. Mr. Art say she sick. Is she okay?"

"She's fine."

"Let me tell you something else on the low-low. My girl, LaQuinta, she works in payroll, say Mr. Art still paying your mama. He must got a thing for her because Mr. Art is a cheap mother, you know what I'm saying. He's got his favorites, but everyone else he treats like crap."

They came to the end of a hallway. "His door is open. That means he ready for you 'cause he usually keep his office door shut. And when he ain't here, it's locked tight."

"Thank you," he said to the receptionist before going into Arthur Davis's office.

"Hello, Drake," Arthur said, getting up from behind his desk and closing the door behind Drake. He shook Drake's hand. "Have a seat."

Drake dropped into the worn leather chair opposite the man who'd threatened his mother. He immediately sensed that Glenda had reason to fear him. It wasn't just the man's tall, powerful frame that was intimidating. He was a dangerous gangster in a businessman's clothing, and Drake wasn't fooled by his duplicitous appearance like Little Red Riding Hood fooled by the wolf in her grandmother's clothing. "Mr. Davis, I know you're a busy man, so I will get straight to the point. It's really simple: Glenda doesn't want to work for you."

Arthur reared his head back and laughed. "She told me that her boys call her by her first name. You never called her Mama or Mother?"

"Mr. Davis, I didn't drive all the way over here to discuss family titles."

Behind dark glasses, Arthur stared at Drake for a moment before removing a bottle of whiskey from his desk drawer. He poured some into a glass that was already half-filled with the amber brew. Arthur drank some of the whiskey. "Things are never as simple as they appear to be."

"What's the complication?"

"She knows too much."

Drake frowned. "How is that possible?"

"I trusted her."

"So now you threaten her?" Drake posed in an indignant voice.

"That was the whiskey talking."

Drake ignored the remark. "Just let Glenda go her way and you go your way."

"Or else what?"

"My intention in coming here was to amicably resolve this situation. I didn't come here to threaten you, Mr. Davis. I don't care about your business—legal or illegal. I don't care if this whole business is a front for some other activity."

"That's what I'm talking about." Arthur banged his fist on the desk. "She knows too goddamn much. As long as she's working with me, I know she ain't going to risk her neck because she'll go down with me."

"I don't play games, Mr. Davis. If anything ever happens to Glenda, you'll be suspect number one."

"Who the hell do you think you are, threatening me?" Arthur angrily uttered.

"I made a simple statement. You can take it how you like," Drake said in a no-nonsense tone.

"You have no idea who the hell you're talking to." Arthur reached into his desk drawer and removed a gun.

Fear rushed through Drake's veins, unsure if the gun was an intimidation tactic or an immediate threat. The fact that Arthur's eyes were hidden behind dark glasses increased his uneasiness, but Drake maintained his composure. He smoothly said, "I went to college with Howard Paulson. He was a couple years ahead of me, but we were cool." Drake stood. "In fact, I was in his wedding party."

Keenly listening for the sound of the trigger cocking into position, Drake stepped toward the door. He turned the knob, only half-convinced that his mother's boss wouldn't shoot him.

Fourteen

From exasperation to
frustration to desperation

Leanne Mitchell forgot about the debts piling up, strangling her business affairs and straining her personal finances. She forgot about the calls from creditors. She forgot about the meeting with her personal banker, in which she pleaded for an extension on her loan. She forgot about her pending divorce. She even forgot about the will, and the woman who wouldn't sign the paperwork.

She forgot about the swirling doom in her life because of Graham's swirling tongue. His tongue was feasting on her most sensitive spot, making slow, deliberate rotations, bringing her closer to the very brink of orgasm.

"Graham!" she cried out.

Graham slid on a condom and then face-to-face, hip-to-hip, he thrust inside her. Not slow, but fast, hard, almost forceful movements. Over and over again, faster and faster, harder and harder until she left the precipice of carnal pleasure and moved into the cavern of orgasm.

For a while they lay quietly still, still joined. Until she spotted the alarm clock and remembered her afternoon tea with Aunt Josephine. "Oh, no, I have to get dressed," she gasped.

Graham gently rolled off her and pulled the sheets over him. "Where are you going?"

"I'm having tea with Aunt Josephine. She hates it when people are late."

"Which aunt?"

"My mother's sister."

"Is she going to bail you out?"

"I don't want to ask for help," she said, walking into the adjoining bathroom. "If I do, I'll have to explain everything."

She came out of the bathroom thirty minutes later, dressed in a floral-print Laura Ashley dress. "How do I look?"

Leaning against the headboard, Graham looked up from the *Wall Street Journal* he was reading, and started laughing. "It's a lovely dress, but not you."

"Graham, I have something to tell you." She opened a dresser drawer and removed a string of pearls. "I followed her."

"Who?"

"That woman who won't sign the papers."

Curiosity aroused, he folded a section of the newspaper. "You did?"

"She lives here now," she said, slipping pearl earrings on her earlobes. "I followed her into a convenience store one day. I tried to start a conversation with her, but she wasn't very responsive. I didn't know what to say. I surely couldn't say, 'Please sign those damn papers so I can get my money.'"

"Of course not."

She moved to the bed. "I even thought about slamming into her car."

"Leanne, were you going to kill her?" he asked, astonishment in his voice.

"The thought ran through my mind. She was sitting at the light and I was driving toward her. I speeded up so I could bump into her and make her crash into the car in front of her."

"What stopped you?"

"I couldn't totally control the outcome." She eased down on the bed next to Graham. "I could have been hurt."

"Most likely you would have." Fingering her blond curls, he said, "I'm glad you didn't."

With her most sad-eyed look and childlike voice, she asked, "Graham, would you help me?"

He watched her lips move and heard the words that came from them. He wasn't sure if really understood the meaning behind her words. His eyes reconnected with hers. "Help you do what?"

"You know what I mean," she half whispered.

"I cannot believe this weather," Satin said, stepping on the running board of Drake's Ford Expedition. It was a beautiful, temperature-setting day. "I talked to my father yesterday. They're snowed in up there."

"The mild winter is one good thing about Atlanta. But summers can be brutally hot," Drake said. "Glenda swears she'd be several shades lighter if it wasn't for the sun. She's always telling my brother and sister-in-law to keep their kids out of the sun. It's impossible down here." Drake hesitated a moment before closing the door, pondering whether or not to kiss her.

"Why are looking at me like that?"

His hand sat on the passenger door, in position to shut it, but motionless. "I'm just admiring your beauty."

Blushing, her lips spread into a self-conscious smile "Thank you."

Drake shut the passenger door and went around to the driver's side.

"Why do you call your mother Glenda?" she asked as Drake drove away from her apartment complex.

"That's her name," he wryly said.

"You know what I mean."

"She had us when she was young and didn't want us calling her Mama or Mommy or anything denoting motherhood."

She detected anguish in his voice. "And that bothers you."

He looked at her for a second. "Yes," he succinctly said. "And she's a trip. A real trip."

"How many kids does your brother have?" she asked, deciding that this was not the time to probe into his relationship with his mother.

"Two. A boy and a girl, Lane and D.J. They're good kids," he said with a tender smile. "Damon and Alanna have a solid marriage. Probably one of the best marriages around. We all met in college."

"What school?"

"Atlanta all the way, baby," he answered with a chuckle. "Damon and I went to Morehouse. Alanna was at Spelman."

"I didn't venture far from home. I went to Case Western."

"That's a pretty good school."

"I had planned to go straight to law school, but I got a great job offer after graduation. I started going part-time last year. I plan to look into law schools around here."

"Georgia State has a reputable law school."

"I'll have to remember that."

"You're off to a good start at work. Randall is very

impressed with you." He angled his face to make eye contact. "I'm very impressed, too."

"Professionally or personally?"

"Both." Drake pressed his foot against the brake, stopping at the red light. "Especially personally." He gently kissed her on the lips. The sweetness of her lips led to a succulent, probing kiss, ending when a horn blasted from the car behind him.

Returning his attention to the road, Drake stepped on the gas. "They're probably talking about us."

"Saying 'They don't look like teenagers,'" she said, giggling. "'They ought to know better than kissing in broad daylight.'" At the next light, the car behind them pulled beside them, positioning to make a right turn. Satin turned and caught the driver's reprimanding gaze and wagging finger. It was an elderly couple, and the wife was driving, hunched over the steering wheel.

"Zandra would do something wild to shock them, like pull up her blouse and flash herself."

"That'd be okay with me," Drake said, grinning at her.

She grinned back. "I'm sure it would be."

"But you would never do anything like that."

"No. I was always Miss Goody Two-Shoes."

"There's nothing wrong with that."

"It's not being a good girl that bothers me," she explained. "It's my friends and family's definition of me. It's limited, as if they can't see anything beyond the good girl stereotype."

"Now you want to be wild and free."

"Free, not wild, and never out of control."

"Like Zandra?"

"She's always been free-spirited. She was real wild in college. No one could believe we were friends because we're so different. We'd go to parties together, but hardly ever went home together."

"What does that mean?"

"I would go home, but not Zandra. I'd leave early and be home in bed asleep before one o'clock."

"So that night we left the club and went for a carriage ride and you got home at three was unusual for you."

"Very."

Drake turned off Interstate 285 onto Cascade Road, heading toward his house. "Are you sure want to go motorcycle riding?" Drake asked. "We could do something else."

"I'm positive!" she gushed. "I've always wanted to ride a motorcycle. My brother has one, but he would never let me ride."

"So you want to do something wild, huh?"

"I prefer the word *unusual.*" She suddenly laughed. "There's that song," she said, hearing "If I Were Your Woman" playing on the radio.

"That's not the first time I've heard it since that night," Drake said. Every time he heard it, Satin seeped into his thoughts. The recurrence was as uncanny as the frequent instances of seeing or hearing the word *satin.*

"I've heard it twice since then." Every time Satin heard the song, she remembered what she did that night. How out of character it was for Cleveland Satin, but in tune with the new Atlanta Satin.

Drake pressed his garage door remote as he pulled into his driveway. "Are you ready to ride?"

"Can't wait!" she answered.

They went inside and donned motorcycle protective gear—helmet and gloves. Drake rolled the Harley-Davidson out of the garage. He inspected the bike and checked the gas gauge.

Twenty minutes later, they were riding on the back roads, heading to a bike riding trail.

The wind whipped around her face, almost burning her skin, but it didn't bother her. She expected to be a little afraid, but her fears disappeared in the wind. She felt as if she were flying, at one with the wind. She closed her eyes and let the sensation take over, enjoying the exhilaration.

By the time they returned to his house, she was convinced that she wanted a motorcycle.

Satin removed her helmet, still breathless. "Remember in the movie *Independence Day* when Will Smith said, 'I've got to get me one of these.'"

Drake grinned at her. "One ride and now you want to buy a bike."

"I know I have a lot to learn about motorcycles and riding, but it was so . . . so exhilarating."

"As exhilarating as this?" He reached for her, pulling her against him with the force of a thunderclap. The kiss he ground upon her mouth was as intoxicating as the wind that whipped around them as they rode. He moved his hands to her face, increasing the intensity of his kiss.

Heat emanated from him, pulsing through his veins, seeping to his skin. His sexual desire seeped into Satin as she responded, realizing the lingering ache in her soul was discontent. His desire became hers, spreading through her—becoming a sweet, aching need for . . . passion.

Passion—that strange achy feeling—took over as she curled her fingers into his shoulders and arched against him. His mouth left hers to seek the hollow of her neck. She released a deep moan, leaning her head back as she welcomed the erotic feel of his lips along her neck.

The good-girl voice protested. *No, no, no. Don't let*

him take you there. Don't give in. The good-girl voice
turned into a wisp of a whisper when Drake slid his
hand under her blouse. He touched the fullness of
her breasts and then tenderly stroked her nipples.
Soft moans escaped from Satin's lips.

Satin wanted to feel his lips close around her nipple.

Drake wanted to lave her nipples with his tongue.

Suddenly his telephone rang. Seconds later his
pager beeped. They were jolted back to reality.

While Drake went into the kitchen to answer the
phone, Satin went around the corner into the bathroom. She freshened up and then stood there,
looking at the stranger in the mirror. The woman she
was becoming and wanted to be was staring at her. But
her reaction of embarrassment was the old Satin. She
wasn't ready to consciously admit how much she enjoyed what she was feeling.

Drake knocked on the door. "Satin, are you okay?"

"Yes," she said, coming out of the bathroom.

"That was my brother. My nephew fell out of a tree.
They had to run him to the hospital."

"Is he seriously hurt?"

"Damon doesn't seem to think so. But I'm going
to the hospital to see him."

"I understand."

"I'm sorry for—"

"Me, too."

"Don't misunderstand. I'm not sorry for kissing
you," Drake said. "I want to make love to you, but not
like that."

She nodded.

"I'll take you home and then go to the hospital." He
walked back into kitchen and opened the garage
door, Satin moving behind him.

In the garage, he opened the passenger side door of his Ford. "You never did answer my question."

A puzzled expression formed on her face. "What question?"

"Was the ride as exhilarating as my kiss?"

"You never gave me a chance to answer."

Smiling, he kissed her again. It was a short, sweet, sensitive kiss, but it wrought the same tremulous effect to their hearts.

"No," she answered when his lips left hers. "There's no comparison."

"Layla! Layla! Layla!" Satin screeched, running into her cousin's outstretched arms.

"Satin! Satin! Satin!" Layla squealed.

The cousins hugged, their mutual affection evident in their bubbly expressions.

"Finally, you have time for me," Satin dramatically said, extracting herself from the embrace.

"Don't even try it, cuz," Layla said. "You canceled our first lunch."

"You canceled the next," retorted Satin, while conducting a visual survey of the spacious office decorated with beautiful artwork and contemporary furniture. "Your new office is beautiful."

"Thanks," Layla said, moving a pile of papers from the sofa. "Have a seat. I'm under a deadline, so there's paper everywhere." She gestured around the room. "As you can see."

"Still Messie Bessie," Satin teased.

"Still neat as a pin?" inquired Layla.

Satin shrugged, as did Layla. They both laughed.

"You look good, girl," Satin said. "I like that suit," she said complimenting the black knee-length jacket and matching cuffed pants that made Layla appear even taller.

"I try. Atlanta's a glamour town." Layla fingered Satin's front layer of curls. "That haircut looks too good. It gives you such a sophisticated, chic look. I know your mama almost died when she saw it."

"She cried. I mean she literally cried." Satin pressed against the corner of the sofa and crossed her legs. "I wasn't there when Daddy told her I was moving. I probably would still be in Cleveland if I had."

"I can't believe you're here."

"It's your fault."

Layla's dark face crunched into a scowl. "My fault?"

"You kept sending me your hot magazine, *Women of Vision*, with stories about women with power and influence. You were subliminally calling me."

"Right," Layla said, giggling. "I just want to know why you didn't get married. I know there's got to be some drama to that story."

"No drama. Just the honest realization that I didn't love Troy. Not enough to marry him. Not enough to be with him for the rest of my life."

"I know that story." Layla stood. "You want some tea."

"Sweet tea?"

"Just the way Aunt Maggie makes it."

Satin grinned. "Oh, yes, I do."

Layla stepped to her office doorway. "Nicki, can you bring us some tea?" she asked her receptionist.

"So, you're all settled on your job?" Layla asked as she turned back to Satin.

"I love it. I like the people. The work is challenging. My boss respects me. He doesn't micromanage." Satin gestured with her hands. "I'm loving it."

"That's great. I'm glad it's working out for you."

Layla returned to the sofa. "Meet any interesting men?"

"I didn't come here looking for a man—that's the last thing I wanted. But . . . I have met this brother. He's fine and he's ooo la la." Satin stopped to laugh.

Layla laughed with her. "Ooo la la?"

"This is going to sound even sillier, but he gives me butterflies. You know that Michael Jackson song?"

"Mmm-hmm, from his "Invincible" CD. He's got you going, huh? I've got to meet this brother. Who is he?"

"Drake Swanson. He's part owner of Marketing Missions, a marketing and advertising agency."

Layla's eyes grew wide. "I know him. And he's a together brother. But let me warn you, and don't be offended, but he's got this player-player reputation. Plenty of sisters have gone after him, but he don't give them any action."

"I know," Satin said, nodding. "Ordinarily I would run from somebody like him, but . . . I'm drawn to him—"

"Like a moth to a flame," Layla teased. "I'm quoting a line from a song by Michael Jackson's little sister, Janet."

"Touché," Satin remarked.

"So you know that he was engaged to Tavia Beaudeaux?"

"The movie star?"

"She left him at the altar," Layla said. "Just be careful, okay?"

Satin nodded. "How's everything with the magazine?"

"Wonderful! My ads are up and we're available on more newsstands—" she said, stopping when Nicki came in carrying a tray holding two glasses of iced tea and a plate filled with pastries.

160 *Robin Allen*

Satin noticed the strange expression on Nicki's face when she placed the tray on the cocktail table.

"Satin, this is Nicki. She's my right-hand man."

"Hey," Nicki complained, "the last time I looked I didn't have anything dangling between my legs."

"She's a local actress." Making eye contact with Nicki, she said, "This is my cousin Satin."

"Nice to meet you," Nicki said, smiling warmly.

"You, too," Satin said. "Thanks for the tea."

"Holler if you need anything else." Nicki deepened her voice to sound like a man.

Satin laughed. "She's a trip!"

"She is," agreed Layla. "What do you think of that trip of a will? Cutting out the men in the family."

"Aunt Maddie was always strange." Satin sipped some of the tea. "You're the only one who hasn't bugged me about signing the paperwork."

"I'm sure you have your reasons."

"The twins are tripping big-time. They keep calling me."

"Your stalling has upped the ante."

"That wasn't my intention. I just want to keep my little piece."

"I hear you," Layla said.

Satin detected a tone of disappointment in Layla's voice. "Everything okay with you?" she asked, glimpsing the shadow of worry on her cousin's face.

"Girl, do what you got to do." Layla's eyes became distant. "We all do what we have to do."

"It's going to be resolved soon. The executors of the estate sent me a letter the other day. I have an appointment to see one of the attorneys."

Upon Satin's departure, Nicki went into Layla's office. Her boss was typing on the computer. "She seemed really nice," Nicki said. "You two probably got into a lot of trouble growing up."

"I couldn't wait for summertime when she'd come down."

"So why you front like that? Why didn't you tell her about this?" Nicki dropped envelopes on Layla's desk from the United States bankruptcy court.

Releasing a frustrated sigh, Layla glanced at the envelopes. "This is a temporary setback. We'll recover. We're going to get some ads. And Pepsi might advertise with us."

Resting her hands on her hips, Nicki saucily asked, "Are you saying that inheritance money wouldn't help?"

"Of course it would." Layla leaned back in the chair and met Nicki's concerned stare. "Especially that third offer."

"So tell her."

"I can't." Anguish and despair reverberated in Layla's voice. "What if my aunt hadn't died? What if that rich woman she worked for hadn't willed her that land? I started this company with very little capital and it doesn't seem right—"

"You know what my grandmother used to say. 'Pride goeth before a fall.'"

Fifteen

Drake wants more than kisses
and Satin learns what bliss is

"Companies always rush to meet yesterday's deadline and maintain quality," Drake said to several of his staff. "And Monet Cosmetics is no different."

"You don't have to give us the quality-but-fast speech," Brent said. "It's our normal mode of operation."

"Too true," Shana said.

"That being said, we have to shift some priorities and start working on the Monet Cosmetics ads," Drake said.

"What's our budget?" asked Brent.

Drake looked around the table with slow deliberation. "Money's not an issue."

Shana's mouth dropped open. "It's not? We have a blank check?"

"Not completely blank. They want to see what we come up with first," Drake explained. "Design three different ads. Be creative, daring, even funky. Think out of the box. That is, don't let costs control creativity."

"This is unbelievable," Brent uttered joyfully.

"Of course, when we present the campaigns, we'll detail the costs and let them decide from there."

"I'm envisioning the glamour look of the future." Brent's voice was full of enthusiasm. "High-techish, chromatic, lots of glitter, and— "

"That's whack," Shana said, moving her hands in a dismissive motion. "It has to be high glamour and glitzy." She pursed her lips together. "Maybe an island theme. Or something with copy like 'Who's that in your mirror?'"

"Not bad," Drake said.

Account executive Marcus Owens looked from Shana to Brent. "I can't envision ideas. I'm very visual, so you have to show me what you're talking about."

"We have to appeal to their market and consider their branding techniques," Drake said.

"So we need to come up with something wicked and cool, but not out of control," Shana said.

"Yes," Drake said.

"What does she mean?" Marcus asked with a puzzled look on his face.

"We'll have to show you," Brent said, chuckling.

"Remember, Tavia is the focus of the ad. The tone should be trendy and edgy, and sexy and provocative."

"Hmm, we can be out-of-the-box creative. We don't have to worry about money. We get to work with a famous movie star." Rubbing his chin, Brake shot Drake a questioning gaze. "This is all too easy. What's the catch?"

"We need comps by next Wednesday," Drake answered.

"Wednesday!" Shana cried.

"That's not enough time," Brent pointedly said. "We have to brainstorm ideas, decide on the approach, find materials, research costs—"

"We'll need pictures of Tavia," added Shana.

"Like I said, everyone's rushing to meet yesterday's deadline." Drake rose from the conference table. "That's it, I'm going back to my office. Come see me if you have any questions or concerns. Don't come to gripe. We don't have time for griping."

Drake left the conference room and went down the hall to his office. A large vase of red roses rested in middle of his desk. Opening the card as he sat down, Drake's eyes widened when he saw the signature: "Tavia Beaudeaux."

"Tavia," he whispered as a range of emotions returned him to the past. Love—how he'd fallen in love with her. Lust—how he'd lusted for her. Hope—how he'd hoped their love would last. Hurt—how hurt he'd felt when she'd left him at the altar. Anger—how love had turned into anger. Bitterness—how bitterness remained in his heart.

Whenever Tavia's name was mentioned, Drake would feel the full onset of those emotions. A year or two after the wedding, it would take him a long time to get to the bitterness, love overpowering the darker emotions. But as time passed, hurt, anger, and bitterness overshadowed love, evaporating the love he'd once felt for her.

But there was something different this time. His memories took him to that unforgettable moment— abandoned at the altar—but he didn't stay there. Instead of dwelling on what had happened, his heart took him to a different place. A place that was pushing away old emotions and making room for new ones. A place that was discovering new rooms in his heart. A place that was making more and more room for Satin.

Drake moved the flower arrangement from his desk to the sofa table. He then decided to send some flowers to Satin.

* * *

"I had a great time," Satin said as Drake pulled into his driveway. "Those comedians are so crazy. They'll say and do anything."

"I'm glad you had a good time. I always enjoy being with you." His hand on the door handle, he said, "Let me get the door for you." He went around the vehicle to the passenger side and opened the door.

She stepped out of the car. Her car keys were in her hand. "And thank you again for the flowers. They're beautiful."

"You're welcome again." He rested his hands on her shoulder. "I really wanted to pick you up," Drake said. "That's the gentlemanly thing to do."

"We wouldn't have made it to the show if you had to come get me. We would have been so late."

"And you hate being late." A teasing smile was on his face.

"Zandra wasn't kidding when she told me Atlanta's traffic is a nightmare." Satin started walking to her Explorer.

"I don't want the night to end. Please come inside." She turned back to face him, uncertainty on her face.

"Have a nightcap." His mouth said one thing, but his eyes raked over her body communicating something different.

"It's kind of late."

"It's Friday night. You're not working tomorrow, right?"

She shook her head.

"Stay for a little while." He resisted the urge to touch her face and kiss her lips, deciding to wait until she was inside the house.

Satin didn't want the evening to end, either. Maybe

it was the enigmatic message attached to the flowers that he'd sent: "Look forward to feeling the essence of your soul. Look forward to discovering the boundaries of your heart."

Or maybe he just wanted to find out where lust would lead. "Just one drink," she said.

One drink later, Satin rose from the sofa. She suddenly began to fear what she was feeling. What would happen if lust became bliss and bliss became happiness? Would she lose control? "Thank you for the drink, but I need to go."

"You can't."

She gave him a bewildered look.

"You're under the influence. In the state of Georgia, you can't drive while under the influence of alcohol."

"I'm fine, Drake," she said with a short burst of laughter. " I can drive just fine."

"In good conscience I can't let you drive. I made that drink very strong."

"It was just wine."

"Georgia cops don't care. If they happen to pull you over and smell any kind of alcohol, you'll be in trouble. I don't want that to happen to you."

"So call me a cab."

"I don't trust taxi drivers. I've heard some strange stories."

"Well, then, drive me home."

"You won't have a car in the morning," he said, standing. He lifted her hand to his face and kissed the back of her hand. "Besides, I think I'm way over the legal limit. I'm under the influence."

"No, you're not."

"Yes, I am," he said, running his fingers along the

curve of her neck and tenderly kissing the softness of her skin. He cupped her face between his hands. "I'm under the influence of you." Then his mouth crushed hers. He could hear his own heartbeat raging in his chest as he ravaged her lips. His tongue explored the recesses in her mouth, discovering softness, sweetness.

He released his lips from her mouth but held her close. "I want to make love to you. I need to make love to you," he whispered. "Can I?"

Desire gripped her as if it had claws. Desire claimed her from the top of her head to the heels of her feet. Desire commandeered the sane part of her brain. Desire was in full control. There was only one way to escape from its grip. Surrender.

She could only whisper "Yes."

"Let's go upstairs," he whispered, taking her hand and leading her to his bedroom. With each step taken, their desire grew. Moonlight filled the bedroom from the skylight over the bed.

Before they made it to the bed, his arms went around her, met at the center of her back, and drew her against him. Their mouths met in a ravenous kiss. His hands traveled down her neck and probed the inside of her blouse. Discovering that she was braless, he caressed her breasts. His fingers curled around her head and then he ravaged her mouth with a kiss.

It was a carnal kiss. It had a dark soul that ignited sparks like the burst of flames erupting from an oil fire—hot, intense, fiery—a fire that accelerated out of control.

"Can I undress you?" Drake breathed into her ear.

"Yes," she said thickly.

He wrapped his hands around both sides of her blouse, and then yanked it apart. Fabric ripped. Buttons scattered. Sequins rained down. Neither cared. He opened his eyes wider to behold her breasts—full, brown-tipped, delicious-looking. He kissed her breasts, stroking the tips with his tongue, drawing them into his mouth.

Moaning, Satin felt faint from the intensity of pleasure. It curled under her breasts and crept down to the cleft between her thighs.

Releasing her breast from his moist mouth, he cried, "You're so damn beautiful."

He ripped his shirt apart, unbuckled his belt and removed his pants, watching as she unzipped her pants and shimmied them off. "Allow me," he said when she slipped her hands into her underwear.

Drake ran his thumb lightly back and forth over her nipples. He covered her breasts with his mouth and slowly slid his hands inside her underwear. On his knees, he planted kisses from her belly button to her bikini line. Her panties between his teeth, he slowly pulled them down to her feet as whimpering, wanting sounds came from Satin's mouth.

He parted her thighs. His tongue discovered her soft, sensitive spot. He tasted her moistness, sending spirals of desire that went straight to her head. "Oh, Drake," she cried. "What are you doing?"

Rising, he planted more kisses on her lips. "I'm going to take you to ecstasy," he promised, circling her breasts with his finger. "Then I'll fulfill your fantasy." In seconds he was out of his shoes and socks, leaving his clothes scattered on the carpet.

"Drake." She gasped short, choppy breaths as he pulled her against his warm, hairy nakedness. Their mouths came together in a passion-driven kiss. He slid one of his hands between her thighs and entwined his fingers in the soft hair, then slipped them inside.

Her fingers encircled his sex, and she caressed its velvety tip with the ball of her thumb.

"Can I feel the inside of you?" he said, reaching for a condom.

Those words felt like he was already there.

He guided his sex into her moist, oval opening. For a split second, Satin saw the cosmos explode. She crossed her legs around his torso.

He began slowly, all the while kissing her on the lips, ears, neck, chin, breasts, anywhere his hungry mouth could reach while he thrust steadily in and out, in and out.

Beneath him, Satin writhed and lifted her hips to meet him, and so harmoniously were they fused that they achieved that perfect syncopation in which man and woman become one. Dazzling sensations washed over her, made her buoyant, sent her rising and dipping through passionate waves of oceanic swells.

"Drake," she moaned, feeling the rising tides of orgasmic pleasure.

"Can I make you—"

Their tempo increased, riding higher and higher, until the waves crashed against the shore of their emotions, and pleasure came raining down like manna from heaven.

They lay quietly, eyes unfocused, waiting for their thundering hearts, runaway pulses, and rapid breaths to return to normal. Before falling asleep, the same thought entered both of their minds: *I will never be the same.*

Satin opened her eyes and stretched her arms across the bed. Drake wasn't there. Memories of their last hours invaded her mind, bringing a wide smile to her face. She'd felt passion—the pull of passion, the pleasure of passion, the power of passion. Now she knew why she'd felt so restless and incomplete with

Troy. He'd never taken her to the land of passion—
the place where physical pleasure and emotions
intermingled. It wasn't a place of fantasy or only for
storybook heroines to discover. It was real. It was raw.
It was riveting.

She'd experienced a sensual awakening.

And she wanted more of it.

Satin got out of bed and went into the bathroom to
wash up. Spotting Drake's robe on the back of the
door, she slipped the robe on and went downstairs.
Nearing the kitchen, she observed Drake as he prepared breakfast. The table was already set. Just the
sight of him sent chills down her spine. Watching
him, she realized that last night wasn't just a surreal
experience, it was an entrée into a new world. Another realization dawned: She could fall in love with
him.

Not now, she chided herself, *not now.* "Good morning," she said, making her presence known.

He looked up and greeted her with that melt-your-
heart smile from their first meeting. But there was
something different in his smile. Somehow she felt
she was no longer on the outside of his heart looking
in, but was on the inside of his heart looking out. And
he was inside her heart. "Good morning, love," he
said. "How are you?"

"I'm not the same," she said, and then kissed him
on the cheek.

"Neither am I." His words were spoken with tenderness and understanding.

She sniffed. "Smells good. Can I help?"

"Have a seat. It's almost ready."

She sat down at the table already set for breakfast.
Looking at the television, which was set to a local news
channel, she listened as the news anchor recounted
the week's top news stories. Drake set down their

plates and joined her at the table. Each plate had an omelette, sausage, and toast on it. Glasses of milk and orange juice had been poured.

She tasted the mushroom-and-cheese omelette. "It's delicious," she said.

"Thanks."

"Is breakfast your specialty or can you cook other things?"

"I cook almost anything. Pops taught us how to cook. By the time we were eleven or twelve, we knew how to cook dinner."

"I'm not into cooking, but I can cook the basics. The kitchen was my mother's domain." She sipped some orange juice. "So, do I lose Brownie points?"

A confused expression was his answer.

"I've heard Southern men like women who cook." Drake laughed. "It's not a big deal to me."

Satin flicked her eyes to the television. "I met him!"

Drake reached for the remote and turned up the volume. They listened to the news report about plans for building a new shopping center in Rome County. A fifteen-second news clip showed developer Jacob Murphy's press conference announcing the shopping center's new design.

"How do you know him?" Drake asked when the news segment ended.

"I had lunch with him."

"Why?" he asked, his eyebrows creased together. "That is, if you don't mind telling me."

"It's a long, complicated story."

"I'm listening."

"Aunt Maddie, my great-aunt, died last year. She had a will that nobody knew about except for Aunt Maggie, her twin. Aunt Maddie worked for a wealthy white family here in Atlanta. She was the maid, cook, and nanny. Anyway, the woman she worked for died before Aunt Maddie died. The woman—her name was Susan Mitchell—bequeathed some of her property to Aunt Maddie. Well, Aunt Maddie willed that land to my cousins and I." Satin nibbled on her toast. "Only female cousins were named in her will."

"Why only females?"

"Aunt Maddie never married. She hated men." Satin responded to the puzzled look on Drake's face. "The story was the man she fell in love with jilted her. She never got over it."

"That's a sad story." Drake could identify with the woman's pain—he knew the anguish of an unexpected ending. But he decided long ago not to let one experience impact the rest of his life. "Where is the land?"

"Apparently where that shopping center is going to be built."

"That's very interesting," he said.

"Last year, I received some papers from the law firm handling Aunt Maddie's estate. It was an offer to buy the land from us. All my cousins have signed the papers, but I haven't."

"Why? Not enough money?"

"Everyone looks at me like I'm a crazy old woman when I say I just want to keep the land." She further explained the events relating to her inheritance, ending with her meeting with Jacob Murphy. "He offered me more money to sign. Not just what I would get from the estate."

Astonished, he asked, "And you turned it down?"

"It didn't feel right, so I didn't do it."

"What happened after that?"

She lifted her shoulders. "I haven't heard from him."

"They can't start building the shopping center until they have title to the land. Yet Jacob Murphy just unveiled a new design at a press conference." He tightened his lips. "Something doesn't sound right."

"I don't want to stand in the way of my cousins getting their money. I'm hoping that maybe a deal can be made that allows me to keep my little piece of the land."

"I don't think it's that simple."

Nodding, she tapped her lips thoughtfully.

"Satin, that shopping center has been big news for a while. It's in a county that's experiencing tremendous growth. Atlanta keeps expanding its borders, so to speak." His voice grew grim. "I'm sure there are people or investors who have put a lot of money into that shopping center. They're going to be quite angry if they lose money because the deed to the land is in probate."

"I never thought about it like that," she grimly said.

"Right now, there are probably some behind-the-scenes players who are getting anxious if this deal falls through. You don't know what's at stake for them and what they'll do." He paused, carefully choosing his next words. "This is a serious situation that can become dangerous."

Her eyes widened, the brown pupils floating in a sea of white. "You're scaring me."

"I don't want to scare you. I'm just letting you know the situation." The possibility of something happening to her frightened him, striking at the core of his fear. "I think you should get in touch with a lawyer right away."

Damon was making some wild dance moves: flailing his hands in the air, jerking his body back and forth, bobbing his head up and down. Alanna unsuccessfully tried to mimic her husband's disjointed, erratic movements. The couple didn't care that they were the subject of finger-pointing and hushed laughter—they were having a good time.

The song changed, so Damon and Alanna stopped dancing and moved away from the makeshift dance floor in the center of their basement. "It's my birthday! It's my birthday!" he chanted while walking toward Drake and Satin.

"You would act this way when I bring somebody over for you to meet," Drake said, slapping his brother on the back.

"It's my birthday. I can be crazy," he said.

"Now he's showing off," Drake said to Satin. "Okay, birthday boy, I want you to meet Satin Holiday. Satin, this is my crazy, wild, goofy, big brother."

"Hello," she said, extending her hand. "Happy birthday!"

"Girl, we are not in corporate. If Drake brings you to my house, I gots to give you a big, old hug." He embraced Satin and then introduced his wife.

Alanna also greeted Satin with a warm hug. "Welcome to our home. Can I get you anything?"

"No, thank you."

"I have to go check on the food," Alanna said. "I'll be back."

"So, Satin, you must be that stripper Drake's told me about?"

A deep crease formed between her brows. "What?"

Drake gave his brother a hard look. "Damon, man!"

"Don't get upset. Let me finish my story," he said to Drake, and then looked at Satin. "You left a hell of an impression on my brother. All he knew was your name. I teased him that you must work for a strip club."

Drake's features knotted in annoyance. "Satin, don't listen to him. He's been drinking."

"Listen now: He wanted to meet you so bad that he called 411 to get your number."

Unsure if she should believe Damon, Satin gave Drake a puzzled look.

Drake was getting perturbed. "You have such a big mouth."

"Here's my point: Drake don't pay much attention to women. They go after him, but he's never interested. Then you come along and he's calling 411. And you meet again at the same place." Damon sputtered in laughter, one hand covering the bottom half of his face. "Is that what you call destiny?"

Satin's puzzled look disappeared with the realization that Damon was trying—albeit awkwardly—to tell her something positive. She smiled. "I don't know."

"Man, now you're getting corny," Drake said.

"Glenda's here," Damon said, observing his mother strutting their way.

Drake put his hand on Satin's shoulder. "Don't let my mother unnerve you. She's very . . . very different."

"I have to meet the woman with Drake," Glenda said upon reaching them.

"Glenda, this is Satin Holiday. Satin, this is my mother."

A questioning look appeared on Glenda's face. "That's not a stage name, is it?"

Satin's answer was succinct. "No."

"I'm so happy to meet you." Glenda draped her arm around Satin's shoulders. "You are a very pretty young lady. And from what I hear, you're real smart."

"Thank you," Satin said, returning Glenda's warm smile. The black leather skirt outfit Glenda wore was something her mother would never wear. It was too bold and funky even for Satin. "Drake's told me a lot about you."

"Good or bad?" Glenda then dismissed her question with a careless wave. "I don't want to know. Come have a sit-down with me and let me tell you some stories about him," she said with a smile and sly wink. "He's smart as a whip and he's got a sensitive soul. He's loyal, too, even when . . ." Glenda's voice trailed off as they stepped into the crowd, their conversation absorbed by the loud music.

Satin cast a sideways glance at Drake.

"Don't look like that, man," Damon said. "Glenda isn't going to run Satin away."

"Get me a beer."

"I'm the birthday boy. You get me a beer." Damon sounded indignant, but really wasn't.

Drake walked over to the bar area and picked up two bottles of beer, opening them before rejoining Damon.

"Remember when I told you I was worried about Alanna?" His voice turned serious as if he'd flipped a switch, going from light to dark.

"Yeah?" Drake recalled the awkwardness of that conversation: he couldn't reveal what he knew. But it didn't matter much now. Alanna's tests were negative. Her symptoms were a reaction to some new medicine she'd been taking. When she called with the news, Drake wanted to stand up and cheer.

"Everything's all right now. She was worried because she had to take some test—" Something in his brother's face made him think the information wasn't new to Drake. "Did you know about it?"

"About what?" Drake gave his brother a what-are-you-talking-about look.

Damon shrugged. "It doesn't matter anyway. I'm just thankful she's all right. When she told me what was going on, I almost cried." He sipped his beer. "Just the thought of losing her makes me crazy. I couldn't deal."

Drake patted Damon's back. "It's all right."

"I'm so glad I never accused her of tipping out. She would have been hurt, especially since she was trying to spare me."

"Big brother, it's your birthday. Everything's cool. Your family loves you. You're working. Don't worry. Be happy." Drake angled his head to view Satin across the room. They shared a smile. "For you, Damon. Don't worry. Be silly."

"I'm cool, I'm cool." Damon drained the remnants of his beer and then turned to Drake. "You've fallen for her. You do know that."

Silence was his answer, along with an oblique look.

"Let me make myself clear. You're not falling, you've fallen," Damon emphatically said.

Damon noticed his father across the room talking to Alanna. "Is that Pops over there with a woman?"

"Ms. Velda Mae Robinson," Drake said.

"You met her?"

"Wait until you see how he acts with her. You'll be saying the same thing about him."

"He's falling?" Damon asked.

"Fallen."

Sixteen

The delusion of illusion

"Knock, knock!" Satin stood outside her boss's open door.

"Come on in," Randall said, beckoning with his hands.

"You're eating lunch. I can come back."

"I'm finished." Randall folded up the wrapper containing the remains of his fast-food hamburger. "Come in and have a seat."

Satin went inside and sat in a chair opposite Randall's desk. "It's so beautiful out today. I still can't get over this weather. I'm enjoying not having to wear a big bulky coat and heavy boots."

"I'm from Columbus, Ohio, so I know how brutal winter can be up there." Randall dropped his fast-food bag in the trash can before getting up to close his door.

An uneasy knot formed in Satin's stomach when the door shut. She didn't know why Randall scheduled the meeting. The E-mail he sent was vague and brief, the subject box empty. His E-mails were usually lengthy and detailed.

Satin considered using a lighthearted approach: a casual, "what's up, boss?" to get a feel for the purpose of the meeting. A smile would mean good news, a frown would signify bad news.

But she decided not to make the first move.

Randall didn't waste time getting to the point. "I want to make you aware of some pending changes that will affect the company and your job."

Satin drew her eyebrows together as a replay of getting laid off ran through her mind. She sighed and braced herself for the worse.

"First things first, and please be aware that this information is highly confidential," Randall explained.

Satin nodded, detecting excitement in his voice.

"We're going to merge with CommunicationsLink. They're based in California. They're more established in some of the markets we'd like to go after." Randall's features expressed eager anticipation. "We're in the midst of negotiations, but it's a 90 percent done deal."

"This is quite unexpected." Her tone was neutral, uncertain whether the news was good or bad.

"We're not going to announce the merger until everything's been finalized. Certain people are being told in advance."

She nodded again, traces of a frown on her face.

"Once the merger is announced, rumors will start flying and people will jump ship. We don't want everyone to leave. Frankly, we can't afford for that to happen." Randall picked up his mug and sipped from it. "Associates who hold critical positions are being told confidentially to assure them that their job will not disappear with the merger."

Satin quietly absorbed the information. The traces of a frown turned into a half smile. "And my position has been deemed critical?"

"Definitely!" he said, smiling. "You've done an excellent job getting the product launch on target, especially in such a short period of time. Your work has not gone unnoticed or unappreciated." Randall jiggled the ice in his cup. "I'm glad I hired you."

"It's been a wonderful experience so far."

"And rest assured that your job will be maintained. There may be some organizational and staff changes, but your role will remain and probably be expanded."

A smile of relief spread across her face. "I'm glad to hear that."

"A lot of things are still being decided, but you might have to relocate to California."

Her eyes widened. "Relocate?"

"Nothing's set in stone. It may or may not happen, but I need to know if you would consider it."

"Permanently?" Her face was a visual display of shock and disbelief.

He shook his head. "It would be temporary, maybe six or nine months. The amount of time depends on the product you're assigned to."

Satin didn't immediately respond. A plethora of thoughts raced through her mind—reasons to relocate and reasons not to. She discounted some of the reasons to not relocate, but the most compelling reason: Drake.

She didn't want to leave Drake, not when they were just beginning to form a relationship. It was much too soon. But maybe not, she thought. Maybe the forces of life were intervening to protect her from future pain. Ending the relationship before their hearts were intertwined like Siamese twins joined at the hip, before the union had fatal afteraffects.

As quickly as she considered that possibility, she summarily dismissed it. There was something special about their relationship. If the relationship ended now, they might not ever find out. And, she wanted to find out why Drake had turned her heart inside out.

She had to know why Drake was as ever present in her mind as oxygen in the air.

"I can do it," she said, expressing the right amount of enthusiasm. Business survival dictated that she respond affirmatively. This was not the time to sound doubtful. After all, she could always change her mind.

"Again, this is confidential, so don't share this information with anyone," Randall cautioned.

"I won't."

Benjamin Reed burst into Jacob Murphy's office. He slammed the door shut and walked over to Jacob's desk. Medium height, stocky built, Benjamin's face was red with anger. "Why didn't you tell me we don't have title clearance?"

Jacob ran his hands through his hair. Reluctantly, he met his partner's furious gaze. "How did you find out?"

"Don't answer my question with a question."

"You don't like dealing with administrative details," Jacob said. "I thought the requirements for the paperwork would be resolved by now."

"What's the problem?" Benjamin plopped down in a chair.

Puffing his cheeks and then exhaling slowly, Jacob explained the problem surrounding title clearance: how Susan Mitchell bequeathed a percentage of the land to her maid who, in turn, willed the land to her relatives. How the woman's daughter challenged the will and how one of the maid's relatives wasn't signing the paperwork, preventing the estate from selling the land.

"Are you saying this project is in jeopardy because of one woman?"

"Satin Holiday. She's an attractive woman."

Benjamin narrowed his eyes. "What does that mean?"

"I met with her." Jacob swallowed. His throat was dry, his mouth sour, the pit of his stomach clenched and raw. He reached into his desk drawer and removed a bottle of Pepto-Bismol tablets. "I offered her a signing bonus—off the record—but she turned me down."

"Are you out of your mind?" Benjamin bellowed. "That was crazy and—"

"I ran it by Paul to make sure everything was legal. He drew up the paperwork, but she didn't go for it. She's not money hungry. I don't know what it would take to get her signature." Jacob popped a couple of Pepto-Bismol tablets in his mouth. "Paul tried to get a judge to grant temporary right of way but it was denied. If this project doesn't kill me, Richard Creighton will."

"He's a cut-throat bastard." Benjamin's lips tightened into a thin line. "I don't trust him."

"Neither do I." Elbows propped on the table, his hands were clasped together. "I had a meeting with him." Seeing the surprise on Benjamin's face, he explained, "I didn't tell you about it. I thought I could handle him."

"But you couldn't," Benjamin stated, not expecting a response.

"I was nervous about meeting him. It was very clandestine." A grimace expressed his distaste of the man. "He basically demanded that we do whatever it takes to start building that shopping center. He's got other deals pending that are dependent on this one." Jacob paused, and then added. "He says that he's the committee. Most of the money is coming from him."

"That changes things."

"I know."

"We don't want to make him mad," Benjamin murmured uneasily. "Hell, we better not make him mad."

"I don't like the idea of falsifying records, but I'm trying to go through the back door. That can always come back to haunt us." Jacob plopped more Pepto-Bismol tablets in his mouth. "And we'd be the fall guys. Creighton would claim no knowledge."

"I've sunk all my money into this and you're at your financial limit." Benjamin banged his fist on the desk. "We can't even bid on anything else right now."

"I want to bid on that Quarterman project," Jacob said, pointing to a thickly bound proposal on the corner of his desk.

Benjamin was silent for several minutes before he spoke. "You should have told me, Jacob." His voice had a razor edge to it.

"I know," Jacob said in the tone of a child chastised for misbehaving.

"If you can't handle this, I will."

Jacob raised his eyebrows. "What does that mean?"

"I'm not going to lose everything—my house, my business, my wife, my family—over a signature!" he said, incredulity ringing in his tone.

"How are you going to make her sign it?"

"Why won't she sign it? What does she want?"

"I don't know. I had an investigator check her out."

"What did he find out?"

"Nothing much. She's not married, she doesn't have kids, she's close to her family. She recently moved here, but there don't seem to be any skeletons in her closet."

"Let me handle it from here," Benjamin quietly said.

Jacob stared at his partner, and then waved his hands in a defeated gesture. "All right."

"You've been the good cop," Benjamin said, ris-

ing from the chair. "I'm going to be the bad cop."
He walked to the door. "If necessary, I'll be the dirty
cop."

Seventeen

Containing the past, present and future

"They've made a decision," Drake said upon striding into the conference room where Shana, Brent, and Marcus were anxiously waiting to find out which ad campaign Monet Cosmetics had selected from the three samples they'd submitted.

"I can't believe they decided so fast," Shana said.

"Neither can I," Brent said.

"You're going to be surprised." Drake poured water into a glass and returned the pitcher to the tray in the middle of the conference table. He sipped some of the water. "Very surprised."

"Don't keep us in suspense," Brent urged.

Marcus snapped his fingers. "I think I know which one."

Shana gave Marcus a curious frown. "But I thought you didn't know."

"I didn't." Marcus looked from Brent to Shana. "I just figured it out when he said 'Very surprised.'"

"Which one, Marcus?" Drake asked.

Marcus swiftly gazed around on the room. All eyes were on him. "'If I Were Your Woman,'" he said with a confident smile.

Shana flicked her eyes on Marcus and then Drake. "Really?"

Drake slowly nodded. "That's the one."

"I just knew they were going to pick the space one. It's edgy and bold, very futuristic and stylish at the same time," Brent said, slightly disappointed. "A lot of the videos have that futuristic feel and high-impact makeup."

"It was too edgy. Even though we're targeting a younger market with this campaign, Monet Cosmetics doesn't want to alienate their base," Drake explained.

"If that's the case," Brent said, "then the other campaign was too cool, too hip-hop."

"Yeah, too ghetto-fabulous." Shana cackled.

"That's one way of explaining it," said Marcus. "I can understand their thinking. Some of their older, middle-age customers might stop buying their products if that went to that extreme."

"Exactly," Drake said. "That's why they chose 'If I Were Your Woman.' That title is familiar to their over thirty-five buyers. But the art treatment is very contemporary and stylish, sexy, yet classy. And that's what they like—the right blend of sexy and classy."

Brent cupped his hand to his mouth before clearing his scratchy throat. "So they can appeal to both markets."

"The subliminal message plays to men and women," Drake said. "For men, teasing them with the thought of Tavia as the woman in their life —"

"Lights up their fire," interjected Marcus.

"And for women, the message is wear Monet Cosmetics makeup and you can have the same kind of sex appeal."

"In their dreams," Marcus said, laughing. "All the

makeup in the world won't help these women look as good as Tavia."

"Please! It's no different than the men believing they're going to sleep with Tavia," Shana said in a defensive tone.

"It's subliminal," Drake said, chuckling. "By the way, the copy is brilliant. Who came up with the concept?"

"It was . . . collaborative," Shana said, "but very much influenced by the Gladys Knight song. We were listening to the radio and brainstorming some tag lines when the song came on. I played off some copy from the hook and Brent did his thing with the creative and somehow it came together."

Drake laughed. "That song is haunting my life." He noticed the strange expressions on their faces. "Not in a bad way. Definitely not in a bad way. Maybe I'll explain it one day."

"Does it have to do with Tavia?" Realizing that she'd ventured into personal territory, Shana covered her mouth. "Oops, I probably shouldn't have said that. I just—"

"Shana, don't worry about it," Drake said. "And I do know everyone's been talking. It's not a secret that Tavia and I were supposed to get married. But that was a long time ago and has nothing to do with today. The past is . . . past."

"Did she have any say in selecting the ad?" Brent asked.

Drake grinned. "Indeed she did. She agreed one hundred percent with Monet's creative team. And it's a good thing they all agreed, or we'd be putting together another set of comps."

"Thank goodness we don't have to do that!" Shana murmured. "I want to go home early some nights."

"So what's next?" Marcus asked.

"We schedule the photo shoot." Drake paused for effect. "In two weeks."

"That's so exciting!" Shana widened her eyes. "I can't wait to meet her! Don't worry, I won't act starstruck."

Looking pensive, Marcus asked, "Brent, did you get copyright clearance on the title?"

"Titles don't get copyrighted," Brent answered. "Lyrics, yes, but not titles."

"That's why there are so many songs with the same title," Marcus thoughtfully said.

"Just to be on the safe side, let's run it by Legal," Drake said. "We don't want to get sued."

"If my opinion matters, I like Satin. I like her a lot," Glenda said, retrieving two glasses from Drake's kitchen cabinet. "So do you."

"I can't dispute the truth." Drake opened the cartons of Chinese food—his mother's surprise dinner as was her unexpected knock at the door. "This looks good, Glenda."

"I'm not going to ask you a bunch of questions about her or what your plans are. I'm not going to tell you to hold on to her or serve up any motherly advice." She laughed and murmured, "That's funny, motherly advice from me. Sometimes I crack my own self up." Glenda placed two soda-filled glasses on the table. "Be happy. If she makes you happy, I'm happy."

"I'm happy," he simply said.

Glenda finished setting the table, laying out plates and silverware. "I got you that seafood egg roll you like. I told them to put in extra lobster."

"Thanks. And your timing is perfect because I was getting hungry and didn't know what I was going to eat."

"Where's Satin? I know you've been seeing a lot of each other."

"She had to go California on a business trip," he answered, thinking about her canceled appointment with the attorney. Kissing her good-bye at the airport, he didn't reveal his concerns about that shopping center or the importance of her signature on certain papers.

Glenda filled her plate with rice, butterfly shrimp, and chicken chow mein. "Whatever you said to Arthur must have scared him to death," she said, pouring soy sauce over her food. "He cut me loose."

"He's a dangerous man." Drake would never tell her about the gun or about the bone-numbing fear he felt walking out of the office. It wasn't until he was inside his car that he allowed the fear to register in his mind and the realization that he'd just made a mortal enemy.

"I told you he's no joke," Glenda said. "Back in the day, he was a numbers man. If too many people played a number that hit, his number runners were known for making people forget what they played."

Drake ate some of his seafood-stuffed egg roll. "How do you know him?" he asked with a reproachful tone.

"We went to high school together," Glenda airily answered. "We kind of messed around back then, but nothing serious. He had a mean streak about him back then and a bad reputation." She reached over and touched his arm. "What did you say to him to make him back off?"

"Two words. Howard Paulson."

She blinked her eyes rapidly. "Who is he?"

"He's an assistant district attorney. He tried that rape case last year against those teenagers who raped that young girl."

A deep scowl claimed Glenda's face. "Those boys needed to go to jail for what they did to that girl. They should have put them under the jail." She scooped some food onto the fork. "How do you know him?

"We went to Morehouse together. You've met him. I think you met him at Damon's wedding."

Chewing her food, she shrugged.

"I really wouldn't want to get Howard involved in something like this, but I was letting him know that if anything went down, he was going to be investigated."

"That's the last thing he'd want." She sipped her soda. "I rented a booth again at Barbara's shop. I don't work on Mondays and Tuesdays, but I'm busy as hell when I'm there."

"Why don't you get your own shop?" Drake suggested. "I'll help you financially."

"Baby, I don't want that responsibility," she said, waving a hand in the air." I don't care about being the owner. I don't want to have to keep up with other folks' money and pay for the place." She tilted her head to one side. "I just want to do folks hair and go."

"Let me know if you change your mind," Drake said.

"I know how you feel about me, and you still help me when I need you." A serious expression on her face, Glenda softly asked, "Why?"

"What kind of question is that?" Drake said, shrugging his shoulders as if could shrug away the memories the question provoked. "You're my mother."

"You say the right things, you do the right things, but I can see that anger sometimes in your eyes." Glenda stared into Drake's eyes. "You can't hide it."

Her honest perceptions brought a grimace to Drake's face. "I can't help how I feel. Like you said, I try to do the right things."

"But I was never a very good mother. I know that. And I know it bothers you. It always did. Even when you were little," she said sadly. "Damon and Derek, they've always accepted me with all my flaws and weaknesses." She paused to laugh. "I got plenty of flaws, I know." Glenda reconnected her gaze with her son's, regret shining in her eyes. "But you, you never accepted me. You always wanted me to be the perfect mother. That's not me, baby. I don't have that mother gene." Her voice softened and she stroked his hand. "I wasn't trying to hurt you or anyone else."

"What's done is done," he succinctly said.

"You've done very well. You're a success. And I can't take credit for it. Roosevelt's a good man and a good father. He raised you well."

Drake nodded.

"So when are you going to forgive me?"

He gave her a bewildered look. "Forgive you?"

"Forgive me for being me," Glenda said, sadness in her voice.

"Are you ready?" Drake yelled from the bottom of the steps.

"I'm coming." Satin appeared at the top of the stairs wearing a red halter-style gown that outlined her figure.

"Hopefully, we won't run into traffic. I know you don't like to be late."

"Let's go." With one hand holding the railing and the other holding her floor-length gown to keep from tripping, she eased down the stairs.

Drake was speechless as Satin descended the stairs, entranced by the vision of ethereal beauty coming toward him. For a second, he wondered, if she was real. Even when she spoke his name he continued to stare at her, drinking in her beauty with his eyes. Feeling her touch his arm and smelling her sweet fragrance, Drake knew he wasn't fantasizing about the beautiful woman in his home and his heart.

"Drake," she repeated, slipping into the power of his gaze. With each step taken, she felt herself drawn to him by a physical and inexplicable force as though he had a powerful magnet inside his chest. Standing face-to-face, the magnetic pull was overwhelming, and threatened to overtake her.

"Satin," he whispered, "you are so beautiful." Taking her face in his hands, he held it gently, his eyes on hers. He pressed his lips against hers, intending to give her a tender, affectionate kiss. His intention evaporated when he tasted her warm, ripe lips.

Satin wanted to say, "We need to leave," but she couldn't fight the magnetic pull of his lips, drawing her even closer. She put her arms around him, kissing him with the same intensity that he kissed her.

It wasn't their first kiss, but he kissed her as she'd never been kissed before, nibbling, devouring, seducing, possessing her mouth. And then his mouth slowly left hers. "We're not going anywhere," he lustily said, looking into her face, waiting for her to protest.

How could she protest when she felt the same way? How could she protest when his kisses sent ripples of desire through her body? How could she protest when his lustful declaration ricocheted from her ears to her heart to the center of her womanhood?

When she didn't protest, he untied the straps of her halter gown, and slowly pulled the fabric down, revealing her breasts. Beautiful, brown-tipped breasts. He traced the curve of her breasts with his fingertip and then gently touched each nipple. "Are you sure?" he asked while caressing her breasts.

"Yes," she softly moaned.

* * *

A few hours later, bodies entwined, sheets tangled, Satin opened her eyes. Drake was staring at her. "You're beautiful," he said.

Smiling self-consciously, she pulled the sheets up to her shoulders. "What time is it?"

"One o'clock. We missed the party."

"I'm hungry."

"I'll see what I can find in the kitchen." He got out of the bed, and went into the bathroom, returning in a robe and holding one for her. "But first I have something for you." Opening a drawer, he removed an oblong box.

Her eyes widened. "A present!" she squealed.

"But first I have a question: Do you believe in love at first sight?" He sat down on the bed.

"I always I thought I was too sophisticated and too intellectual to believe in love at first sight." With a smile sweetened by contentment, she touched his face. "Either I've lost my mind or my emotions have taken over my intellectual thinking."

"I didn't believe in it, either . . . until I met you. You've been a shadow in my thoughts from the very first day I saw you."

"I couldn't forget you, either. What other explanation could there be?" she posed.

Taking her hand to his lips, he kissed her fingers. He opened the spring-hinged lid to reveal a three-tiered diamond necklace hanging from a gold chain. "This is for you."

She gasped. "It's beautiful." She touched each diamond in the necklace, as a host of emotions sailed through her.

"The three diamonds usually represent the past,

present, and future. But these diamonds have different meanings."

"Different meanings?" she marveled in a whisper.

"The diamonds are for my heart, soul, and—"

"I don't know if my heart can take this," she said, her heart beating wildly.

He placed her hand over his chest. "You are the rhythm of my heart."

"Be still my beating heart," she said, entranced by his gaze.

Touching the second diamond, he said, "My soul was lost in darkness until you brought light to my soul."

Unbidden, tears sprang into her eyes. "Be still my beating heart," she whispered.

"And the third one is for love. You made me believe in love again." He tilted her chin and stared into her face—the face he couldn't forget. "I love you."

Her heartbeat was far from still. It thundered with speed and plundered with emotion. With those three words, she knew why. "I love you," she breathed.

His tongue stroked her lips, and then demanded entrance and explored deeper.

Clutching hold of his arms, she met his tongue with her own, and they danced an oral duel to the music in their hearts.

"Are you still hungry?" he asked.

"Not for food," she answered, drawing him on top of her.

Eighteen

*When inheriting land
means inheriting trouble*

"Mr. Washington will be with you shortly," the legal secretary said, leading Satin into the attorney's office. "Have a seat."

"Thank you," Satin said, smiling politely at the older woman with hair dyed a frightening black and lipstick as red as blood.

"Let me know if you need anything," the secretary said before leaving.

Satin surveyed the office: the desk was mahogany, the rug was Persian, the chairs were a rich crimson leather. Hanging on the wall, alongside the bookcases containing voluminous law books, were testaments of the lawyer's educational achievements: bachelor's degree from Emory University and a law degree from Georgia State. The law degree reminded Satin of her dream to become a lawyer, causing her to make a mental note to research the law schools in Atlanta.

She reached into her briefcase and removed several large envelopes—the envelopes she'd received from the law firm representing her great-aunt's estate. Satin remembered the reactions to the first envelope: Both of her twin cousins had excitedly called her at work to tell her about the offer. By the time Satin got home from work that evening, they'd called to find out if she'd received an envelope. The envelope had been in her mailbox, but she hadn't opened it yet. When Satin opened the envelope and read the documents, she was as surprised and excited as the twins. But to her cousins' dismay and utter frustration, Satin decided to proceed with caution. She'd learned from business negotiations and training classes not to take the first offer. So she didn't.

With the counteroffer, Satin realized that owning the land was more important than the money. She hadn't even known she felt that way until she was placed into the situation that required her to make such a decision. Perhaps it was something that her grandfather used to say: "Ownership is power." Or maybe it was something she learned in Economics 101. She didn't know the source of her desire, but felt its surge to retain the land.

Still, she hadn't realized her idealistic views would have such an impact on her relatives.

Even more so, she really had no idea what was at stake for the investors and developers of that property.

"Hello Ms. Holiday. Sorry to have kept you waiting. I'm Barry Washington," the lawyer said, entering the office and extending his hand to Satin.

"Hello," she said, shaking his hand. "Drake Swanson referred me to you."

"I haven't seen Drake in a while," he said while walking to his desk. "I recently read in the *Atlanta Chronicle* that his agency landed some work with Monet Cosmetics." Barry shuffled some papers around and placed a yellow legal pad in the center of his desk, prepared to take notes. "How can I help you?"

Satin wondered if he could. The blond-haired man with blue-green eyes looked like a teenager. Satin glanced at the degrees on the wall and quickly calculated his age to be around forty. She looked back at him and noticed the small grin on his face. But there was a keen intelligence and edginess in his eyes that somehow betrayed his boyish appearance.

"So you've figured out that I didn't just graduate from law school," Barry said, the grin spreading across his face.

Satin responded with a sheepish smile. "Well . . . you look—"

"I know," he said, nodding. "Sometimes my youthful appearance can be very disarming in the courtroom."

"I have a feeling you know just when to use it." She nervously tapped the envelopes on her lap. "I'm not sure if it will help in my situation."

"My youthful appearance isn't my only weapon." Elbows on the desk, he folded his hands together. "Tell me the situation and I'll tell you if I can be of service."

"My great-aunt bequeathed some land to my cousins and I that she inherited from a woman she worked for. Aunt Maddie was a maid and she worked for a woman named Susan Mitchell."

"Her family owns a lot of property throughout Atlanta," Barry said. "Over the years, some of the land has been sold off."

"I don't know the details about this particular piece of land, but apparently it's connected to this big shopping center that's being built in Rome County."

"The Rome Shopping Center."

Satin nodded.

"That's a big development deal. Some major Atlanta investors and developers are involved."

"I don't know about that. All I know is that I received some papers offering $10,000 to sign over the deed. I turned it down because I like the idea of owning land."

"But more offers came," Barry prodded.

"I received two more offers, the last one for $20,000."

"That's a nice inheritance," he said.

"Especially since it was unexpected."

"Your cousins are pressuring you to sign."

Her eyes widened. "How did you know?"

"I deal with wills and estates all the time. Wills can sometimes be divisive, and even destroy a family."

"My cousins are so anxious for me sign the paperwork. They leave me messages almost every day." She paused, uncertain whether or not to tell him about Jacob Murphy's proposition.

"Go on—" Barry encouraged.

"What I tell you has to be strictly confidential."

"Are you going retain my services? I'll have my secretary draw up the paperwork immediately."

Satin studied the attorney's face. Relying on Drake's recommendation, she decided to place her trust in him. "Yes."

Barry pressed the intercom button and directed his secretary to draw up representation papers. "Now that that's been taken care of," Barry said, upon hanging up the phone, "please continue."

"Jacob Murphy—he's a developer—offered me an off-the-record signing bonus." The blank expression on his face changed. "I turned him down."

"Do you know what that means? They probably can't start building until they have the deed to the land. They don't have the title. That's the only reason why Murphy offered you money." Barry shook his head. "That was very risky for him."

"He said our conversation was confidential."

"Of course. My guess is that the investors who put money into the shopping center believed the land was free and clear," Barry said. "Why did you say no? Why don't you want to sell?"

"At first I just wanted to retain ownership of the land. When the offers increased, I figured the land must be very valuable."

"It is," he confirmed.

"If I sell, that's the end. If I keep it, I'm guessing the property will continue rising in value. If it's worth a lot now, how much will it be worth next year or five years from now?"

"You don't know. An economic downturn can have a drastic effect on property value."

"I'm going to be optimistic. I think it will increase." Barry nodded.

"All the paperwork that we get is identical. From what I understand, all of us have to sign or the deal is no good."

"That is correct."

"My cousins want the money. I don't want to stand in the way of them getting their money. So is there any way I can retain the percentage of land that is mine and they get the money for their percentage?"

"That's not typically how it's done."

"Is it possible?"

"Yes."

The possibility of a solution created a smile on Satin's face. "What needs to be done?"

"Let's not get too excited too early," he cautioned, observing the change in Satin's demeanor. "The piece of land that might be deemed your piece might be important for the shopping center. It could be the area designed for the heart of the shopping center."

"I didn't think about that," Satin said, a sigh of frustration coming from her lips.

"It depends on the land that was bequeathed to your aunt. It depends on the specifics in the will that Susan Mitchell left to your great-aunt. And it depends on the terms outlined in your aunt's estate," Barry explained. "So you see, it's not as simple as it sounds."

Satin dropped back against the chair. "Nothing ever is."

"I'll have to meet with the estate attorneys to explore your options."

"Will that take long?"

"It depends. For instance, the estate can offer you another portion of the land, but it has to be of similar value. If other heirs are involved, and most likely they are, it can get sticky. The heirs can protest the change and can drag things out for years. Frankly, I don't think the shopping center development can wait for that."

"So what do you recommend?"

"I'll reserve my recommendations until I've fully investigated the matter and all related issues, but I think you should be aware of the full impact of your decision." His face was solemn, his tone serious. "Do you realize you're putting yourself into a dangerous situation?"

"Look directly into the camera, baby," the photographer directed Tavia Beaudeaux who was seductively posed in a supine position against a red sofa. "Give me that sexy mama face."

Seduction shone on Tavia's face, lust sizzled in her eyes. Although the cream foundation and mascara were as heavily applied as the sparkle-berry blush and crimson-red lipstick, the camera captured the erotic essence of a woman of desire, of a woman to desire, of a woman to desire to be.

"Make love to the camera, baby," the photographer said, clicking and flashing his camera.

Tavia posed, the camera catching a cacophony of come-hither expressions.

"Scene change," the photographer yelled while reaching for another camera.

Tavia extended her right hand, and made a back-and-forth motion with her right index finger, indicating for the photographer come to her. He did as she requested. "Don't call me 'baby,'" she said in a tone of voice meant to belittle.

Celebrity attitude wasn't new territory for the photographer. He knew how to play the "I'm-nobody-you're-somebody" role. "Please forgive, Ms. Tavia, I had no idea you didn't like to be called . . . that word. It was not meant to offend. No, no, no," he said profusely. "I like to give people, my very special people, a special name, a term of endearment—"

Tavia rigorously shook her head.

"Oh, you don't like names like that."

Tavia nodded. "You may call me Ms. Tavia or Ms. Beaudeaux."

The photographer bowed. "As you wish, Ms. Beaudeaux."

Tavia scanned the room, but did not see the person she was seeking. "Where's Drake? Did he leave already?"

"He's here somewhere," the photographer said. "I'll have my assistant get him." The photographer glanced at his assistant who'd also heard Tavia's request. With no exchange of words, the assistant left the room in search of Drake.

"This time we're going for a different vibe," the photographer said. "Before, you were sexy and seductive. Now I want you to be sexually raw. In the heat of passion. This time you're going to be sitting up and leaning forward. Not all the way but just enough to give the impression that you're coming toward the reader." He paused and added, "Ms. Tavia, give me that if-I-were-your-woman-what-you-would-do-to-me attitude."

As the photographer positioned Tavia and the makeup artist touched up Tavia's makeup, Satin was walking through the hotel lobby and down the escalator to the level where the photo shoot was taking place. She stopped in the ladies' room and overheard a conversation that made her heart stop. She didn't know to whom the voices belonged, but she knew who they were talking about.

"Did you see the way he looked at her?"

"Yeah, girl, he's still in love with her."

"They say he was heartbroken when she left him standing at the altar. As fine as he is, I can't see why she did that."

"Oh, you like Drake."

"Yeah, but he's not paying me any attention or anybody else."

"You're late. I heard he got a girlfriend now. He's smitten."

"I guess he *was* smitten. His old flame is back to douse out that new flame."

"Girl, you are so crazy."

Satin remained in the bathroom stall until the women left, their shrill voices ringing in her ear. She waited a few minutes before she stepped out of the stall. She washed her hands, and when she looked in the mirror she saw the tears that had begun to form in her eyes.

She was hurt. *I thought he loved me.*

She was angry. *How dare he treat me this way.*

She was confused. *Why would he invite me to this photo shoot if he was still in love with Tavia?*

Satin blotted her eyes with a napkin. His gift suddenly caught her attention. The three diamonds. She touched the diamonds, remembering what he said each diamond represented: his heart, his soul, and his love. At the moment, they symbolized hurt, anger, and confusion.

Satin left the bathroom, and instead of going to the ballroom where the photo shoot was taking place, she turned toward the elevators. She pressed the up button, but when the elevator doors opened she didn't get in. Instead, she strutted down the hall to the ballroom. She was going to tell Drake what she heard and how she felt. And she was going to demand an explanation.

Inside the elaborately decorated ballroom, she saw Tavia Beaudeaux, her long frame provocatively draped against a red sofa. She was as beautiful in person as on film. A surge of jealousy and fear coursed through Satin. She could reconcile jealousy, but fear of a lingering love was another matter.

The photographer was shooting Tavia with a sexy smile on her face. Satin realized that Tavia wasn't just posing for the camera; she was obviously looking at someone and he or she was making her smile. Satin angled her head to see the subject of the actress's smile. Her heart fell into the pit of her stomach when she saw the object of Tavia's attention—Drake. She didn't think her heart could sink any lower, but it did when Tavia bounced off the sofa and then wrapped her arms around Drake. From her viewpoint, she could see Drake smiling—that smile she thought was hers alone.

Satin stepped back into the doorway. Angry tears brimmed her eyes. She decided to call him—right then. She dialed his cell phone, hoping it was in his jacket pocket. It rang and rang and rang, and then he finally answered.

"Hello," he said.

"Drake," she said, her voice sounding more tremulous than she intended. Her anger, not her pain was what she wanted him to hear. "Are you still in love with Tavia?"

"What? What are you talking about?"

She reentered the room, walking halfway through so that he could see her. Tavia was standing close to him, whispering in his ear. "What is she whispering to you?"

Drake jerked his head away from Tavia and then looked around the room. He saw Satin a few feet away, too far to touch, but close enough to see the anguish in her eyes. He felt it in his soul.

Spinning around, Satin rushed from the ballroom.

"Excuse me," Drake said, looking at the photographer and then Tavia. "Finish up this session without me." He immediately left, but when he entered the hallway he didn't see Satin. He quickly walked to the elevator and pressed the button. Out of the corner of his eyes, he spotted Satin on the escalator, nearing the lobby level. "Satin!"

Their eyes met for a fleeting second and then she stepped off the escalator. By the time he reached the lobby area, she was gone. He called her cell phone several times, but it immediately went to voice mail. She didn't want to talk to him. How long, he wondered, would Satin refuse to talk to him?"

"Wake up, sleeping beauty," Graham whispered into Leanne's ear. "Your prince has arrived."

Leanne slowly opened her eyes and lazily stretched her arms above her head. "My prince is late."

"Late, but with good news," he said, turning the bedside lamp on.

"Graham, please," she said, flinging her hands over her eyes. "Turn the light off."

"I'm not going to tell you the news until you're awake."

"Okay, okay," she said, turning back around. She propped herself up against the pillows surrounding the headboard. "This better be good."

"Oh, it's so good, I know you're going to want to thank me the way I like to be thanked," Graham said, unbuckling his pants.

Her sleepy face turned into a scowl. "I'm not in the mood!"

"What if I tell you that your money problems will soon be over?"

"Only in my dreams." She pulled her knees up to her chest. "Aunt Josephine was explaining why Mama put Maddie in her will when she got sick, and couldn't finish the story." She rustled her blond curls with her hands. "Knowing why won't help me." Her voice became agitated. "I want all that money! That girl has to sign those papers!"

"Her John Hancock won't matter much if she's . . . like John Hancock."

Leanne gave him a blank look. "What are you talking about?"

"Her John Hancock won't matter much if she's . . . like John Hancock."

As comprehension slowly dawned, a smile formed on her face. "You didn't actually ask someone to—"

Graham answered with a broad grin.

Leanne closed her eyes. "I can get my money. I'll be able to pay off that loan. I won't have to close my stores." A new thought jumped in her mind, and her eyes flew open. "They can't trace anything to us, right?"

Graham shook his head. "There won't be nothing to trace. They're going to make it look like a random act of violence."

Leanne laughed wickedly. She scooted over to the end of the bed and then unzipped Graham's pants. "Now for my random act of kindness."

"I told you I had good news."

Nineteen

Drake writes a different ending to his fantasy

Three days had passed since Satin had seen Tavia whispering in Drake's ear. Three endless days and three eternal nights. She refused to see or talk to him. Drake tried calling her at work and at home. He called her cell phone, but she never answered. He E-mailed her at work and at home. He went to her apartment, but she wouldn't answer the door.

He finally received a communication from her. When he opened the Federal Express box he couldn't imagine what was inside. But when he saw the three-tiered diamond necklace—his declaration of love—he knew that she was serious. Hurt and anger claimed his soul. He'd finally let a woman into his heart and—bam!—she ran out of his life from a little misunderstanding. A minor misunderstanding to him, but obviously major to her.

Drake forced himself to concentrate on the task at hand: selecting the best photos from the photo shoot. The photographer had done an excellent job capturing the spirit of the "If I Were Your Woman" campaign. The mood and tone of the shots enriched the high-impact style. Even the black and white photos, which he'd initially resisted, were outstanding.

Drake had to admit that Tavia was stunning. She sparkled with sexiness and sizzled sophistication. She had the look—it had made her a movie star. With several photos spread across his desk, Drake speculated that Monet Cosmetic's creative team was going to have a difficult time selecting the right photo for the ad.

A soft, sexy voice suddenly interrupted him.

Only it wasn't the voice he wanted to hear. The voice belonged to the woman in the pictures he was staring at.

"Can't get enough of me," Tavia said, standing in his office doorway.

His eyes went from her bewitching stare in the photographs to the hypnotic gaze in person. In a glance, he knew what she wanted. A clingy black dress adorned her lithe frame and funky knee-high boots covered her long legs. Diamonds sparkled around her wrists and neck and dangled from her ears.

As she closed his office door and strutted across the room, the word *action* popped into Drake's mind. She had a role to play and he had yet to decide how he would play his role.

"Alone at last," she said, coming around to his side of the desk. She quickly scanned the photos, smiling satisfactorily. "Beautiful. Very beautiful."

"The photographer did a great job."

"Of course, I made it easy for him," she said with a sparkle of laughter. "But I didn't come here to talk about work." She perched on the edge of his desk, facing him.

"I didn't think so," Drake said, allowing his eyes to roam her body. He expected to feel an onset of desire, but for some strange reason, he didn't. His response was benign, almost as if it—the love he once felt for her—had never been there. That was how he felt when they met two weeks ago—a numbness he attributed to the context of their meeting even after many years. They were both working and had roles to play. He was the marketing executive professional overseeing the photo shoot and she was the diva. But now that they were alone, he thought his response would be different. He realized—to his surprise—he was unaffected by her.

"You got something to drink?"

"Sure." He went over to the wet bar and removed two glasses. He dropped ice in the glasses and poured whiskey into each. "This isn't top shelf, but will have to do." He handed her a glass and sat down in his office chair.

"Cheers," she said, raising her glass upward before taking a sip.

They drank in silence, warily watching each other. Drake had decided that he wasn't going to make the first move.

"I'm sorry, Drake," she softly said. "I'm sorry that I did . . . what I did."

"Left me standing at the altar. Humiliated me in front of my family and friends." He sounded angrier than he intended.

"Yes, I'm sorry for that—"

"For what?"

She exhaled, and then met his intense gaze. "I'm sorry for standing you up. I didn't know how to tell you that I had an audition. I tried to get it scheduled for the next week, but I couldn't. I had to take my chances. It was a now or never kind of decision."

"You made a choice. And look at you now. You're a superstar."

"That's not all I want," she said in a patient voice.

"Not happy being admired, not happy being worshiped, even revered," he taunted. "You've made *People* magazine's Most Beautiful list. You're on the cover of every magazine imaginable. You've won awards. You star opposite Hollywood's leading men—"

"Drake . . . I—I just want you to hear my side," Tavia stuttered. "I'm not the coldhearted bitch you think I am. I can understand why you might think that way, but I'm not." She hurried to add, "I really wanted to marry you. What I'm trying to say is that I didn't want to make a choice. I didn't consciously choose my career over you."

"It just happened that way." His unforgiving expression matched his unforgiving voice. He proffered his drink in the air. "To unconscious choices."

"I've always felt guilty about what I did. I hope you believe me," Tavia sincerely said, gently touching his face. A long silence pause followed while she sipped her drink and stared at her former lover. "I truly didn't mean to hurt you. I tried to call and apologize. But you wouldn't talk to me."

Drake scowled. "T.T., there was nothing to say. The damage had been done."

"T.T.," she whispered. "No one's called me that in a long time." She looked into his eyes. "I even called the church to try and reschedule the wedding."

Drake gave her a baffled look. "What for?" he indignantly asked. "So you could do it again?"

"I wouldn't have," she cooed, then slid down the edge of his desk until she was standing in front of him. "I'm really sorry. You do believe me?"

Drake studied her face, but didn't answer.

She smiled at him, the toothpaste-bright smile that enchanted Hollywood and ensnared many fans. "Do you believe me?"

"I believe you," he simply said.

"I've never forgotten about us. I still have feelings for you." She waited for him to say something. "I'm very happy to see that you're doing so well. I never thought we'd be working together."

"Neither did I."

"Maybe it's a sign."

He cocked a skeptical eyebrow. "A sign of what?"

"That we're not finished." Tavia ran her fingers across his lips. She slowly lowered the front zipper on her dress revealing her rather large breasts for her lithe frame.

Drake looked at her breasts—they were beautiful and tempting. How many nights had he fantasized about this moment? In his fantasy—the moment she came to him for forgiveness—he would make love to her: enjoy her delicious body and give her such pleasure that she would scream his name. He had different scenarios for the fantasy, but they all had the same ending—he would leave her as she'd left him.

Staring at Tavia's body, he still felt lust . . . for revenge. He looked at her face and saw remorse. He was convinced of her sincerity, but that didn't change his fantasy. Satin did.

Because of Satin he didn't want to make love to Tavia. Her presence, in fact, reminded him of how much he wanted Satin.

Tavia cocked her legs on each side of his chair and smiled when she saw that Drake knew she was not wearing underwear. "Remember that time we made love outside in the pouring rain?" she purred, and then lifted his hand to her breasts. "Remember when we—"

"You're more beautiful than I remember." He

touched her face. "But let's get comfortable on the sofa."

Half-naked, Tavia moved to the sofa.

"I'll lock the door." Drake headed toward the door.

Sitting on the sofa, her back facing the door, she said, "Help me with my boots."

"I like them on," he huskily said.

"Oooh, I like that," she purred.

Drake quietly opened the door and slipped out his office.

Parked near Satin's apartment building, he waited for her to come home from work. It was 6:25 P.M. and he expected her to arrive soon. Ten minutes later, she steered her red Explorer into a parking spot near the entrance to her apartment. He watched her reach over to the passenger seat for her briefcase and purse. She opened the door and stepped out the vehicle.

She's beautiful, he thought. *With her pretty face, her sexy body, her lovely legs. I want her.* A lecherous smile crept over his face. She was going to be alone this evening. Her roommate was out of town.

He got out of the car and quietly followed her. Not wanting to be seen, he entered from the opposite side of the building. He quickly but quietly went up the stairs. The key was in her hand, positioned for insertion in her apartment lock, when he called her name. "Satin!"

A loud, piercing sound came from Satin's mouth. "No, please don't hurt me!" she screamed. Drake's warning, "You need to be careful," and the lawyer's remark, "You're putting yourself in dangerous position," rushed into her mind bringing an onslaught of fear.

Hands trembling, she tried to put the key in the door, but missed the keyhole. She tried a second time and missed again.

"Satin!"

The voice sounded familiar. It belonged to Troy Moss. Heart pounding, she turned around.

But the familiar face did not evaporate her fear. She remembered the last time she'd seen him: the raw anger on his face. It was still there, even though he tried to hide it with a smile.

"Hello, baby," he said, raking her body with his eyes.

"Hello, Troy," she said, trying to sound casual.

"You look good." He stepped closer. "Damn good!" He kissed her on the lips.

"What are you doing here?"

"I came to see you."

"That's nice," she said, half smiling. "But this isn't a good time."

He crunched his brows together. "Why not?"

"I just got in from work. I can freshen up and meet you somewhere for dinner." Hoping he would agree to her suggestion, she inserted the key into the lock. "There's a great Italian restaurant—"

"Let's go inside," Troy demanded. "I didn't come all the way down here to talk to you in the hall!"

She fumbled with the key, unable to open the door. "I don't know what's wrong with this lock. It jams sometimes. Zandra said she was going to have the lock changed. I don't know why I can't get the key to turn."

"Here, let me help you. I told you I wanted to take care of you. That's all I wanted to do." His voice grew angrier, his face meaner. "I don't know why you did what you did. I was never untrue to you. I was going to take care of you."

"Troy, that's why I don't think you should come in—"

"You humiliated me. Everybody in Cleveland knows you just left me like I was a no-count brother. It's not going down like that." Troy pushed her hands away from the doorknob and reinserted the key. He turned the key, unlocking the door. "Presto!"

"Troy, please don't do this," she pleaded.

"Don't do what? Do this?" He pushed her against the door and covered her mouth with his lips.

She tried to push him away, but his full weight was pressed against her. "Stop!" she cried when he released his lips from hers.

Drake heard a woman's voice as he walked toward the entrance to Satin's apartment building. He wasn't sure whom the voice belonged to until he reached the inside of the building. He ran up the stairway. A powerful surge of anger overcame him when he saw a man pressing his body against Satin. Drake grabbed the man by the neck and yanked him away from Satin. The man stumbled back against the wall and fell to the floor. Drake punched the man several times until Satin urged Drake to stop.

"Call the police," Drake said.

Satin shook her head. "He'll leave. He'll leave."

Troy pulled himself up from the ground. His eyes narrowed at Satin, he muttered, "You done already got you a new man. You conniving . . ."

Drake punched Troy again, knocking him to the ground. Realization suddenly dawned. He looked at Satin. "You know him?"

"Yes," she said, her heart beating rapidly. "He's from Cleveland."

"I'm not just some no-count brother from Cleveland. She's my fiancée." Troy grabbed on to the railing and pulled himself up. "She was my fiancée until she up and left six months ago." Troy stumbled to the stairs. "I betcha she do you the same way."

Satin went into the apartment and plopped supine on the sofa. Drake followed her inside and locked the door.

They were silent for several minutes. Satin waited for her heartbeat to slow down while Drake waited for an explanation.

"Thank you, Drake. Otherwise," she sputtered, "I don't know what he would have done to me."

He nodded, studying her face to determine her emotional state. Within fifteen minutes, he'd felt sadness from missing her, fear upon hearing her scream, anger upon realizing that the man who attacked her was no stranger, and now confusion.

"You never told me you were engaged."

"I don't know why. It wasn't intentional. I just really wanted to forget that episode of my life." She raised her eyes up to meet his inquisitive gaze. "We were engaged. There was never an actual wedding date. It never got that far." With tenderness in her voice, she said, "It wasn't like your situation."

"I came over here to apologize to you. I don't want you to think there's anything going on between me and Tavia." He pointedly added, "There isn't."

"That's not what I heard . . . or saw."

"Yes, Tavia was flirting with me on the set, but that's all there was to it," Drake said. "She was flexing her star power."

"I overheard some of your employees in the bathroom talking about the way you were looking at Tavia. I didn't see who they were, but they think you're still in love with her."

"I don't care what they say," he said, shrugging.

"People like to gossip. But their perceptions aren't my reality."

"You told me how devastated you were when she left you that day," she gently said. "Everyone seems to think that you never got over her."

"That may have been true, but—"

"So . . . I was stepping aside to make it easier for you to—"

"It was true, until I met you. But not now." He walked to the balcony door and stood there in thoughtful repose. "Tavia threw herself at me last night. Came into the office to seduce me. I knew she was going to try eventually. But I didn't allow it to happen. I didn't because my feelings for her are gone. It would have just been sex. But I don't want sex. That's all I've had for years." He turned around, catching her serious expression. "But with you I'm making love. And that's what I want." He walked over to the sofa. "Remember what you said in the club when 'If I Were Your Woman' came on."

She nodded, curiosity gleaming on her face. "All those women were surrounding you. I said, 'If I were your woman you wouldn't want another woman.' I don't know why I was being so bold."

"Your words were prophetic. When Tavia tried to seduce me, that's exactly what I thought. I don't want another woman. I want Satin." He sat. "That's what I came over here to tell you . . . but now I find out that you were engaged."

"I didn't want to marry him because I knew I couldn't be me. I didn't realize I didn't want to marry him until he proposed. He kept pressing me to set a date, but I didn't. I never was excited about marrying him. I didn't shop for a gown. I didn't do all the things you're supposed to do if you're going to get married," she explained, her mind spinning to the past.

"Everybody thought we were the ideal couple. But Troy has to be the big man. My career could never be important. When I got my promotion he wasn't happy for me. He thought I was going to somehow eclipse his career, eclipse his manhood."

"So you left him because of your career. Is it that important to you?" Drake asked, a long-suppressed fear revealing itself.

"My career is important to me. But that's not the only reason why I didn't marry him. He didn't make me feel . . . I mean really feel from inside."

They were silent again, lost in their cacophony of mixed emotions.

"There's nothing going on with Tavia and me."

Satin studied his face, searching for signs of truthfulness. His earnest eyes revealed much emotion.

"You're the reason I walked away from Tavia. That's how serious I am about you."

"I'm serious, too."

"Are you?" he asked, uncertainty framing his face. "And for how long?"

The tone of his question was like a sharp knife pressing against her skin. "I'm very serious," she declared.

Standing in front of her, he asked, "What do you want?"

The wary edge in his voice felt like a knife piercing her skin. "I want to be with you."

"For how long?"

"I don't know."

"Until you get a job offer elsewhere? Until you decide that your career is more important?"

His accusatory tone yielded an expression of distrust that penetrated her heart with the sharpness of a razor's edge. "That's not what I mean."

"Let's cut to the chase," he said. "You know what I ultimately want. A family and kids. But if you're all about your career . . ."

"That's not all I want in life. I didn't marry Troy because I never felt for him what I—I feel for you," she stammered. "That's the difference . . . a big difference."

"Are you sure?"

"Positive."

"Because if you're not sure, I don't want to find out after I propose, or after we set the wedding date," he said with deep emotion, "or on the day of our wedding or after you have our child."

"Drake, I can't say that I'm going to be ready for marriage tomorrow or next month," she said, looking at him. "All I know is what I feel in my heart for you. I have never felt this way before."

"I don't know if I can take the chance that you might change your mind." He gave her a long, thoughtful look. "How do I know you won't change your mind tomorrow or next year?"

She opened her mouth, but no words came out. She didn't know what to say.

"You don't know," he said.

"I can't guarantee—"

"You're right. There are no guarantees. I can't stop you if you decide to change your mind. But I don't have to be there if you have a change of heart," he murmured. "I can prevent it from happening . . . by not being there." He cupped his hand under her chin and stared at her, a tortured expression on his face. "Good-bye, Satin."

Unable to move or speak, she watched him walk to

the door. He seemed to move in slow motion as if he were uncertain of his decision.

Satin wanted to scream, "Please don't go." She wanted to scream, "I love you." In that moment, she realized that she would love him forever and forever. And when he closed the door, tears fell from her eyes. She didn't even know she was crying.

Twenty

Satin takes control and
circumstances spin out of control

"I'm so glad you're here," Leanne drawled when she walked into her bedroom to find Graham lying on the bed.

"You said to meet you here." Viewing her from head to toe, the conservative suit and frilly blouse, the pearls hanging from her ears and dangling around her neck, Graham said, "You look as demure as a schoolteacher." He grabbed her and pushed her down on the bed. "What a turn-on," he said, pinching her lips together and kissing them.

"Stop!" Leanne said, pushing him away and raising herself to a sitting position. "I had tea with Aunt Josephine. She's so sweet. She told me things I wish I knew about. Important things."

Graham leaned against the headboard, one leg propped up. He narrowed his eyes at her. "Like what?"

"The reason why Mama left Maddie that land."

"I'm real curious about that," he said.

"You're not going to believe this." Leanne fidgeted with the pearls around her neck. "Mama gave Maddie the land because she saved my life."

"You're not making sense."

"If it weren't for Maddie I would probably be dead," she declared dramatically.

"Are you saying the maid saved your life?" His tone was full of derision.

Leanne slowly nodded. "Aunt Josephine said that I got real sick when I was a little girl. I kept getting sicker and sicker. They took me to different doctors but they couldn't figure out what was wrong with me. I guess Maddie told them about her special potions and they let her try them." Her voice became a whisper. "My daddy must have thought I was going to die."

"You must have been really sick."

She rose from the bed and walked to the dresser. "A few days later I was out of the bed. Aunt Josephine says it was a miracle and nobody knew what was in Maddie's medicine. Mama used to say I wouldn't be here if it weren't for Maddie, but I never knew what she meant." She removed and dropped the pearl earrings into a dresser drawer, and spun back around. "My daddy didn't want anybody to know that he let the maid give me her special medicines. Aunt Josephine says he told everyone he had a specialist flown in from France."

Graham grinned. "I'm glad she saved you."

"Don't you know what that means?"

Graham's grin reversed itself and became a grim line. "What are you talking about?"

"We can't do anything to Maddie's relatives! I shouldn't have challenged the will. I guess I should have trusted Mama." She released a deep sigh. "She had a reason for willing that land to Maddie. I'm the reason and—"

Standing, Graham extended his right arm and was moving his left arm over his right in a back-and-forth motion mimicking the movements of a violinist. He made loud, screeching noises, mocking violin sounds.

"Graham!"

"How touching," he sneered.

"You don't have to care about my family's past, but I do."

He shrugged and dropped back down on the bed.

"I don't want anything to happen to her. I don't want her hurt."

"Or killed?"

"Don't say that word," she said, covering her ears. "Maddie saved my life. We can't do anything to her niece. It would be . . . wrong."

"The maid saved your life. But that was a long time ago. What does that have to do with today? You still need money, don't you?"

"Yes, but—" She averted her gaze.

"Yeah, but it's too late anyway," he murmured.

Not hearing him, she said, "I would just feel so guilty."

"You don't know how to feel guilty." He studied her face. "There's something you're not telling me."

She tapped her lips with her fingers. "Aunt Josephine says she'll loan me money until everything is settled with Mama's estate."

"Now I understand. You're not afraid of feeling guilty, you don't want to risk certain legal consequences if you don't have to." He pointed his fingers in between her breasts. "It's not guilt, it's fear."

"Maddie did save my life. And I did care for her." She fluffed her blond curls with a manicured hand. "I'm going to get the money I need, so it seems completely unnecessary to go after that girl."

"Like I said before, it's too late."

"What do you mean it's too late? They already . . . did it?" she asked, her voice shrill with fear.

Graham shook his head.

She dramatically fell back against the bed. "So she's okay?"

"At the moment, yes. But it's too late to stop them."

Leanne raised herself to a sitting position. "Call the person and tell them not to do it," she demanded.

"I didn't make the arrangements. I don't know who to call."

Her bright blue eyes widened and her mouth dropped open. "I don't understand."

"I didn't want to be connected or have anything traced back to me so I talked to a distant cousin. He's nobody you'd want to mess with. He told me he would take care of it. I tried to find out how and when, and he said the less I know the better. He said it would look like she was a victim or an innocent bystander. Once it's done, he's going to contact me for payment."

"Call your cousin, damn it!" she urged. "Tell him you changed your mind."

"He told me not to call him. I'm supposed to wait for him to contact me. He's a dangerous type. I'm not about to cross him."

"You chicken! You're scared of your own cousin."

"You'd be scared of him, too."

"You've got to do something," she insisted.

"Can you stop a bullet once it's been fired?" he asked, his hand on her shoulder, his eyes probing her face. "The only thing you can do is get the hell out the way."

"You're going to run away from me before I run away from you," Satin said to Drake when he opened his door. "Is that the plan?"

"I'm not running," Drake coolly replied, although his heart ricocheted at the sound of her voice.

"May I come in?"

He deeply missed her, but resisted the urge to call her. A week had passed—a miserable, lonely week—but he stood by his decision. It was a preemptive move designed to protect him from pain he was already too familiar with. Yet he couldn't deny the joy he felt upon seeing her, but hid it behind a mask of indifference. "Yes, come in."

Satin followed him into the kitchen. "Are you running from me?" she asked, standing in front of the kitchen table.

Drake folded his arms across his chest. "I'm not running anywhere."

"Yes, you are." Smiling enigmatically, she held out her arms to display two small suitcases.

He cocked his head. "Where am I going?"

"You have a choice." She handed him one of the suitcases. "This is the suitcase you'll take if you run from me."

"I'm not running anywhere," he repeated.

"Open it," she softly said.

He reached for the suitcase, and then opened it, thinking how much he missed her. It was better to bear a broken heart now and not a broken soul later. Inside the suitcase was a red heart; her name was scripted across the center of the heart.

"You can run from me," she said in a low voice, "but I'll still be with you . . . in your heart."

He stared at the heart before raising his eyes to look into her beautiful face. His resistance level dropped another 25 percent. He'd already lost 25 percent of his resistance when he opened his front door and saw her standing in the doorway.

"Satin—"

"Open this one," she said, indicating the other suitcase.

"I don't think we should have this discussion. Your career, your dreams, and—"

"Open it," she whispered. "Please."

He hesitated before twisting the suitcase lock. Another heart bearing Satin's name was inside, along with photographs of them, a camera, and rolls and rolls of film. His resistance dropped another level.

"I don't know what the future holds, but I do know that you're in my heart. . . . You've taken over my heart," she said, staring into his face. "I want you in the pictures with me. Where they're taken, who else is in the picture, what we're doing. . . . None of that matters." Exhaling nervously, she sputtered, "What matters is that you and I are in the pictures together.

"Some companies guarantee their pictures. If you don't like them, you don't have to buy them," she continued, her emotions rising. "I can't offer that kind of guarantee. The only thing I can guarantee is that as long as there is love between us, I'll be in the picture with you." Her hand over her heart, she gazed into his eyes. "I plan to love you forever."

Her heart was pounding with the ticking clock, and she waited for him to say something. He didn't speak or move. "So which trip are you going to take?"

Drake stared at her with most intense gaze. The intensity frightened her. Was he angry? Was he offended? Was he disappointed? Was he going to walk her out the door?

How dare you take me there! he thought. *How dare you take me where I don't want to go! How dare you make me feel my fear!* He released a heavy sigh, and faced the simple truth: She was inside his heart.

His gaze softened and Satin realized that it was the

essence of his love radiating from him, almost blinding her with its intensity.

"How dare you make me . . . love you the way I do!" he said, coming toward her, closing the gap between them. He cupped his hands around her face. He kissed her—a raw, primitive kiss. "How dare you make me want you! How dare you make me need you!" He kissed her, biting and nipping her lips.

The kisses sent shock waves through her body. "You haven't answered my question. Which trip are you going to take?" she breathlessly asked.

"I have a question for you." He kissed the nape of her neck, then traced his tongue across her collarbone. "Can you run away from me?"

Understanding that he needed confirmation of her feelings, she looked deep into his eyes, penetrating his soul. "I can't run away from you now . . . or tomorrow."

His resistance at ground zero, he threw the suitcase with the lonely heart across the room. "Does that answer your question?" He unbuttoned her blouse and captured her right nipple in his mouth.

Kneeling, he unzipped her pants and pushed them down her legs. With both hands, he curled his fingers around her silk panties and ripped them apart. He tasted the fruits of her passion, the succulent essence of her womanhood. "Does this answer your question?"

Gripping the arms of the kitchen chair, Satin couldn't respond. The world was spinning, time was spinning, she was spinning into the labyrinth of love, into a world where reality was an illusion, and illusion was reality.

Drake rose, unbuckling his belt and taking off his pants, his eyes fixated on Satin lost in love's labyrinth. He knocked the kitchen tabletop items to the floor, leaning Satin against the table. He placed his hand under her chin and drew her mouth to his. He feathered his lips across hers. "I love you, damn it." Then he grounded her mouth with a kiss of surrender, sweet surrender. "Does that answer your question?"

She didn't need to speak. Her answer was in the bliss of surrender. She kissed him back, fully, deeply, completely.

On top of the kitchen table, he made love to her, beginning with the center of her desire and ending where no ending exists—her soul.

Jacob knocked on his partner's door before going inside. He sat in the finely upholstered leather chair and waited patiently while Benjamin finished his telephone conversation.

Benjamin hung up the telephone, Jacob's broad smile arousing his curiosity. "What's up?"

"I just got a call from the attorney's office. There's been an agreement with the executor of the estate," Jacob said, as gleeful as a child on his first trip to Disneyland. "I don't know the terms of the agreement, but apparently she's agreed to sign the papers they've drawn up. And when she does, we'll finally get title clearance." He excitedly banged his fist on the desk. "We can break ground!"

Benjamin's face became ashen as if were going to vomit.

"I thought you'd be excited. Now we don't have to worry about the Portman brothers stealing that project from us."

"And they were just waiting for the clock to run out. Tick, tock, tick, tock." Benjamin drummed his fingers against his desk. "They were going to sweep that project right from under us." He sunk back into his high-back swivel chair. "And I would have lost everything," he said, desperation in his voice. "Everything."

"I was on the brink of financial despair, too. Saved by the hair of our chiny, chiny, chin." Laughing, Jacob sat back in the chair. "That's all behind us and we can move forward."

"Nicole would leave me. If I go broke, she would be gone. I know it! She's used to living well." Benjamin paused and then mumbled, "I wasn't going to let that happen."

Jacob glared suspiciously at his uncharacteristically subdued friend. Normally Benjamin would be incessantly talking about expected earnings and the next project, and plans for money not yet earned. An uneasy feeling swept over Jacob.

Benjamin stared at the floor. "I wasn't going to lose everything."

"What do you mean?" Jacob got up and went around the desk.

Benjamin raised his head to look into Jacob's worried face. "I wasn't going to lose everything."

"What did you do?" Jacob asked.

"I can't lose Nicole," he mumbled.

"What the hell did you do?" Jacob demanded, shaking Benjamin from his trancelike stare.

"I got in touch with this guy I know. He did some construction work for us a while back. I told him about the situation and he said he would take care of it."

"What is he going to do?" Jacob's voice was shrill with disbelief.

"I told him to rough her up and scare her into signing." Catching Jacob's disappointed look, he said, "I know it was stupid."

Neither spoke for a moment.

Benjamin sighed. "He said roughing her up would make things worse. Silence is golden."

"You should have told him not to do anything!" Jacob shouted. "You should have walked away clean!"

"I don't want to lose Nicole."

"Do you think Nicole is going to visit you in prison?"

Benjamin washed his face with his hands.

Jacob picked up the telephone handset and dropped it in Benjamin's lap. "Call it off! Call it off—now!"

Twenty-one

Danger . . . danger . . . danger, Satin

At the Atlanta airport, Drake waited near the top of the escalator with flowers for Satin. Yawning, he considered taking a seat on the bench near the baggage claim. It was his second trip to the airport, as her plane was delayed. Suddenly, he spotted her coming toward him as the moving stairs drew closer. She looked tired, but smiled upon seeing him.

"For me?" she asked when he handed her the flowers after greeting her with a kiss.

"No one else but you," he said, smiling.

"Thank you, honey." They walked toward the baggage terminal. "I'm exhausted."

"So am I," he said, checking the flashing signs over the baggage carousels for Satin's plane number.

"I don't think the luggage is there," she said.

"Let's sit down," he said, pointing to a bench.

They waded through the crowd and sat down where they could still observe her plane number flash indicating that the luggage from her plane was available for pickup.

"I missed you," she said, resting her head against his shoulder.

"Ditto," he said, kissing her forehead. "How did the meeting go?"

"It was a very interesting meeting."

"Very interesting in a good way. Or very interesting in a bad way?"

"It depends on your perspective. There's been some major reorganizational changes. We're going into matrix management, which means alignment with products."

Drake assessed her face, trying to determine if she might have to relocate. Ever since she shared the news about her company's merger and possibility of a temporary relocation, he worried that temporary would become permanent. He sincerely didn't want to interfere with her career. But could they withstand the challenges of a long-distance relationship?

"Go on," he prodded.

"My product, the one you developed 'Ring, Ring, Ring' for, will be transferred to San Francisco."

"Permanently?"

"Yes, and no."

Drake 's stomach turned. "What does that mean for you?"

"At one clock, California time, all VoiceBox products were going to be handled there. Two hours later, the decision was reversed and one of the senior vice presidents resigned. I was getting a tour of their R&D department when I was called in to a meeting. They decided to keep my products here in Atlanta, but now they want me to launch one of their products. By the way, they really like the work you did."

The compliment did not deflect his main concern. "But that would mean relocation."

"They said temporary, but twelve to eighteen months is a long temporary."

"So what did you tell them?"

"I told them I didn't want to move again."

"And—"

"They suggested I think about it, and made it very clear there was only one position for me. Either I have to take that position or I won't have a job."

"Where was your boss?"

"Mysteriously missing in action." She looked up and saw the plane number. "My luggage is here."

"What are you going to do?"

"I honestly don't know."

"Barry Washington is on line one."

"Who?" Drake's attention was focused on a sales report.

"Barry Washington. He's an attorney."

"I'll take it," he said, remembering that he'd referred Satin to him. He picked up the receiver and depressed the flashing button. "Hello, Barry, how are you?"

"Doing very well. And yourself?"

"Everything's fine with me."

"That's good to hear," Barry said. "I'm calling about the woman you referred to me. Satin Holiday. Is she a good friend?"

Drake answered the question with a question. "Why do you ask?"

"Because the matter we met about is rather serious."

"Her inheritance?"

"Oh. So you know about it?"

"We've been seeing each other," Drake explained simply.

"Good. I'm sort of stepping out of professional bounds here, but I just don't think she realizes the full impact of the situation."

"What do you mean?"

"The developers haven't been able to start building the shopping center because they don't have title to the land. The project has been held up for over a year for various reasons. I've heard they're ready to move posthaste. There's a lot of money tied up in this project and some rather important people are getting nervous."

"What are you trying to say?"

"People do crazy things when they're afraid of losing money."

An uneasy feeling claimed Drake. "Are you saying that she's in danger?"

"I've heard some things."

"Threats against her?"

"Nothing specific. Nothing direct, of course." His voice took on a warning tone. "I know some of the people involved. As an attorney, I'm sometimes privy to a variety of information."

"I understand."

"I know certain people have a lot of money riding on this project and they have a vested interest in seeing that shopping center become a reality. You just never know what people will do." He paused and then said, "I'd be quite disturbed if something happened to her."

"What can Satin do to extricate herself from the situation?"

"I negotiated an arrangement with her aunt's estate. It would be highly improper if I elaborate. Suffice it to say, I think she'll be pleased."

"That's good," Drake said, feeling a spark of hope after the disturbing news.

"She needs to come to my office. I'll explain the terms of the agreement and review the paperwork that she'll sign. She canceled our appointment last week, but she really needs to sign them right away."

Drake tightened his grip around the telephone. "ASAP?"

"Yes."

"Why the urgency?"

"Let me put it this way: Until she signs those papers, she's in danger."

P.F. Chang's was crowded. A lunchtime favorite, the upscale restaurant drew many people who worked in businesses in the surrounding Perimeter area. Three cars deep, Satin waited for a valet attendant to park her car.

Inside the restaurant, she immediately spotted her cousin Layla.

"You're almost late," Layla said, tapping her fingers on her watch.

"Almost," Satin said, shaking her head. "I'll never adjust to this traffic." She sat down and draped a napkin over her lap. "How are you?"

"Fine," Layla answered, forcing a stiff smile at Satin. "Just fine."

Satin parted her lips. A wary look came to her face. "You're lying."

Layla met her cousin's probing gaze and slowly picked up her glass of water. "You know?"

"Yes," Satin gently said.

"Who told you?"

"Aunt Maggie."

"I didn't want her to know." A shadow of sadness covered Layla's face. "She was so proud of me."

"She still is." Satin affectionately patted Layla's arms. "So am I."

A friendly waiter approached the table to take their

orders. Satin viewed the eclectic offerings on the menu. "I don't know what to order."

"I know what you'll like," Layla said, pointing to a dish on the menu. "That's what I always order."

"Looks good. That's what I'll have," Satin agreed, giving the menu to the waiter.

"Same for you, ma'am?" the waiter asked Layla, who responded affirmatively.

When the waiter left, Satin asked, "Why didn't you tell me your business was in trouble?"

"I tried to handle it on my own," she explained. "I've had financial challenges before and something usually comes in from somewhere unexpectedly."

"Like our inheritance," Satin said.

"Something like that."

"Well, something unexpected is going to come your way again."

Layla cleared her throat. "What do you mean?"

"I'm going to sign the paperwork. I have an appointment with my attorney today at 6:00 P.M."

Layla closed her eyes and muttered a quiet prayer. "What happened? What made you change your mind?"

"I went to an attorney and he worked something out with the estate's attorney. I don't know exactly what he negotiated. I'll find out tonight. But I've decided to sign the papers." She raised her glass to her lips. "The twins have been bothering me. Your situation. And that shopping center. I'm getting out of the way." She drank some water and laughed. "If I don't get my forty acres and a mule, then so be it."

"Thank you," Layla said.

"You don't need to thank me." Satin surveyed the crowded restaurant. "This is a very nice place." Rubbing her forehead, she asked, "Do you have any Tylenol or Motrin?"

"I'm sorry I don't. Have a headache?"

"It's been bothering me all day."

"Your message about looking for a job surprised me," Layla said, curiosity on her face. "I thought you liked your job."

"I love my job. But the company has merged with another company."

"So your position has been eliminated?"

"I don't know for sure. That's the problem."

Layla gave her a befuddled look. "Explain that."

"The company I work for has merged with this high-tech company from San Francisco. There's a big power struggle going on. A senior vice president quit last week. My position was supposed to report to the executive vice president in San Francisco, but my boss has been fighting to retain his products," Satin explained. "Right now, my position is here. But next week, I don't know."

"And if the position is transferred to San Fran, what are you going to do?"

"I don't want to move again. I've only been here for six months." Satin paused and her face grew warm. "And . . . I don't want to leave Drake."

Layla heartily laughed. "You are in love."

"Yes, I am," she admitted, grinning.

The waiter arrived with their food. While eating, they reminisced about childhood events, laughed about family stories, and shared their plans for the future.

"And will Drake be in those future pictures?"

Remembering the night she boldly went to his place with the suitcases, and remembering the erotic way he made love to her on his kitchen table brought a passionate gleam to Satin's eyes that Layla noticed.

"Girl, you're thinking about one of those nights," Layla teased.

"Can't deny it," Satin admitted, blushing.

"Speaking of Drake, isn't that him?" Layla asked, pointing toward the front entrance.

Satin lifted her eyebrows in surprise. "That's him."

"I told you I knew who he was," Layla said. "We've just never formally met."

"Hello, ladies," Drake said, before kissing Satin on the cheek.

Satin introduced Drake to her cousin.

"I've seen you around town," Drake said. "Your magazine is excellent."

"Thanks." Layla tendered a subtle suggestion. "It's a great place to advertise . . . Marketing Missions."

"I'll keep that in mind. That really is very good idea." He took a seat at the table. "Right now, I'm on a different kind of mission." He turned to Satin. "Barry Washington called me."

A puzzled expression drew Satin's brows together. "Why did he call you?"

"Who is he?" Layla asked.

"He's the attorney Drake referred me to," Satin answered.

"About?" Layla probed.

"Our inheritance."

"I don't know anything yet," Layla said, "but I get the feeling something's wrong."

Drake detailed his conversation with Barry. "It was an 'off-the-record' conversation. He wouldn't call me unless he had reason to worry. Bottom line is you're in danger."

"No one has threatened me or followed me," Satin murmured.

"You can be so naïve," Layla remarked.

"I'm sure no one has threatened me." She paused, remembering the strange man sitting in an old car in her apartment parking lot. "I haven't received any phone calls or messages saying, 'Sign the papers.'"

"They're too smart to directly threaten you," Layla said. "Somebody could be watching you and you don't even know it."

"You guys are frightening me." Satin shifted her eyes from Drake to Layla. "My head is really hurting now," she said, massaging her temples. "I have an appointment with Barry at six o'clock."

"You're going to stay with me until the paperwork is signed and things settle down." Drake spoke decisively, but looked at her for approval.

"My daddy wouldn't approve," Satin said.

"If her daddy was here, he'd be taking her back to Cleveland," Layla said. "He'd probably hire a bodyguard. Uncle Oliver don't play about his baby girl."

"Let's not panic," Drake said. "We'll go see Barry, take care of the paperwork, and resolve the matter."

Satin released a nervous sigh. "Okay."

The waiter arrived with the check. "My treat, ladies," Drake said, reaching for the bill.

Layla rose from the table and kissed Satin on the cheek. "I'll check on you tonight. And thanks for lunch, Drake. Take good care of my cousin." Layla walked away from the table.

Minutes later, Satin and Drake left the restaurant. "I'll follow you back to work," Drake said. "I parked in the lot." Pointing to the parking lot exit, he said, "I'll meet you over there."

A slight frown formed on her lips. "That really isn't necessary."

Drake wrapped his arms around her in a protective embrace. "Yes it is." He kissed her, then said, "I love you."

"I love you, too," she said, smiling tenderly. "I need to stop at a gas station for gas and some Motrin."

Drake nodded. "Just follow me."

Satin gave the valet driver her ticket and waited while the attendant retrieved her vehicle. She tipped the driver, stepped inside, and turned on the ignition. She drove behind Drake, following him to a gas station.

She stopped in front of a gas pump and got out of the car. She swiped her credit card at the pump and opened her gas tank door.

"I'll take care of this," Drake said, grabbing the gas hose.

"I'm going inside," she said. "I need to get something for my headache."

A look of concern penetrated his face. "Are you sure you want to go back to work?"

"I'm under the gun," she said. "Deadlines, deadlines, deadlines."

Inside the gas station, she surveyed the counters for the medicine section. She traveled up down several aisles. Midway down the last aisle, Satin spotted the counter with pain relievers. Reaching for a bottle of Motrin, she didn't notice two men enter the gas station. A few feet away, they donned masks and approached the store clerk.

"Give me the money in the cash register," a man demanded. "All of it!"

"He has a gun!" a woman screamed.

"Everyone stay calm and no one gets hurt," threatened the second man, waving a gun.

Satin looked up and saw the two masked men in front of the checkout counter. Heart pumping with fear, she ducked down and scooted to the end of the aisle and hid behind the potato chip rack. She couldn't see the men, but could hear them.

"Hell no, we needs more bling-bling!"

"That's all we have!" the clerk cried.

"Then hit up the customers," the other gunman said.

"Whack idea. Naw, man, we ain't got much time," the second gunman said. "Let's get out of here."

"Take this, you cheap-ass store," one gunmen said, shooting out the surveillance camera.

"I've always wanted to do this," the second gunmen said, aiming his gun at the soda fountain. He pulled the trigger. "Bulls-eye!" Moving down an aisle, he saw Satin and then nodded to his cohort.

The gunman opened a cooler door and fired at the cartons of milk. "Bulls-eye!" Milk spilled onto the floor.

The other gunmen fired at the rack of chips and then randomly shot around the store.

A bullet struck Satin.

His back facing the store's entrance as he pumped gas, Drake turned at the sound of gunfire. Two masked men were running out. He dropped the gas hose, leaking its flammable contents.

His heart racing, Drake rushed into the store. "Satin! Satin!" he screamed.

"There's a woman down back there," someone said.

Drake ran to the last aisle. Almost slipping on the spilled milk, he rushed to the end of the aisle. Satin was lying in a pool of blood.

"Somebody call an ambulance," he yelled.

"Baby, where are you hurt?" He dropped to the floor and gently touched her face.

"In my back," she groaned.

"An ambulance is on the way!" someone yelled.

"It . . . hurts," she moaned.

Drake felt helpless and frightened. "I'm here," he said, trying to keep fear from his voice. "I'm right here with you. You're going to make it. You're going to make it." He kissed her. "Say it with me: I'm going to make it! I'm going to make it!'"

"I'm going to make it," she whispered.

"You're going to make it," he repeated.

"I'm going to make it," she weakly whispered.

"I love you so very much," Drake said.

"I love you, too," she said, her eyes half-closed.

"Don't close your eyes. Don't leave me." He squeezed her hands. "You're going to be all right!"

"Smile for me . . . the way you did . . . when we first met," she uttered in ragged breaths.

Smiling was the last thing Drake felt like doing. But it might be the last thing he could do for her. As soon as that thought entered his mind, he immediately chased it away. Yet, struggling against his deepest fear, he forced a smile on his lips. It came from a force within, a force with its own power. His lips, empowered by that mysterious force spread into a wide, reflecting smile. It radiated his love—his life force.

Satin's eyes flickered and she returned his smile—for a whisper of a moment—and then her eyes slowly closed.

Twenty-two

You were my woman

It was a mercilessly hot day. It was the hottest time of the day when doctors recommend people remain indoors or seek the shelter of shade. But there weren't many shade trees in the cemetery.

Doctors couldn't dissuade him from his destination. He parked his car and stepped out of the cool air-conditioned vehicle into the sweltering heat. Sadness, not heat, dizzied his soul. He felt the depth of his sadness with every visit.

But emotion wasn't going to deter him from his destination. There was no place to hide from himself or her—she was ever-present in his heart.

He walked along the shoe-trodden path, but could find his way without the trail. His heart was his guide. He'd traveled the path in blistering heat, gusty winds, and driving rain. Weather conditions never discouraged him.

Reaching his destination, he placed a bouquet of flowers on her grave. He ran his fingers across the name etched on the tombstone.

"You were my woman," Wilbur hoarsely whispered. "You always will be."

Epilogue

Twelve months later

The woman in the mirror was wearing a delicate lace veil. Her makeup was flawless. Her shoulder-length hair was full of loose, bouncy curls. She wore an elegant wedding gown. A blissful smile was on her face.

The woman in the mirror was Satin Holiday.

She smiled at herself. *I'm getting married.*

Sitting in the church's dressing room, Satin couldn't help thinking about the past year of her life, the events that led to this very moment. So much happened, so much changed, and so much remained the same. It was a year of self-discovery and courage, a year of miracles and love.

Images of the past year whirled in her mind. How a robber's bullet almost took her life, and the miracle of her recovery. How the light of Drake's smile and the power of his love formed a path for her to find her way back to the living. How—days later—she opened her eyes to see her family and Drake's family surrounding her with their love and support.

It was a momentous year in other ways. A year in which she explored options, but decided that relocating again was not an option. So she turned down the high-profile position in San Francisco, and found a new job—working for the same boss, but with a different company.

It was a year in which she discovered new options. Choosing not to sell her portion of the land she'd inherited from Aunt Maddie turned into an unexpected opportunity. In lieu of the land, she was offered a small partnership in the shopping center. It was an offer she couldn't refuse.

Nor could she refuse Drake's marriage proposal. It was a romantic encounter of the unforgettable kind. An evening that began and ended with surprises during a weekend trip to Las Vegas. It began with an invitation-only dinner at an elegant supper club and Gladys Knight singing "If I Were Your Woman," dedicating the song to "Satin Holiday and Drake Swanson." Later that evening, Satin and Drake returned to their hotel room. There was a knock at the door. Satin opened the door and screamed when she saw singer Brian McKnight standing in the doorway holding his guitar.

"I guess you have the wrong room," she said.

Smiling, he entered the penthouse suite. "Are you Satin Holiday?" he asked.

Satin was speechless when he began to sing "If I Were Your Woman" with a different twist: "If I Were Your Man." Sitting against a red divan, she felt every beat of her heart as Brian McKnight sang: "'If I were your man, this you must understand, that what we have is divine, and I will love you until the end of time.'"

Shortly after the award-winning singer finished his serenade, he left. Satin knew that something even more special was going to happen. Indeed, it did. On bended knee, Drake proposed: "Will you marry me?"

Her heart thumped with joy, the rivers of her soul

grew still. There was no hesitation in her response. Every fiber of her being screamed, "Yes!"

A week later, Satin had booked a wedding planner and identified places to have a reception in Atlanta and Cleveland. She immediately began searching for her wedding gown.

Indeed, the gown she wore was beautiful. Wearing it, she would marry the man who melted her heart with a smile. And not a moment too soon. Her brush with the claws of death taught her to respect the fragility of life. Life had no guarantees other than to live in the moment—fully and completely. She intended to share many Kodak moments with Drake.

"Satin, are you okay?" Zandra asked, interrupting her reverie. "You have a funny look on your face."

"Just thinking," she answered, smiling. "Just thinking."

"Happy thoughts," Zandra said, fingering the delicate veil. "It's your wedding day. Only happy thoughts allowed."

"You do look beautiful," Kendra said. "You real lucky that bullet didn't scar your back or you wouldn't be wearing a gown like this."

"Why would say something like that?" Zandra chided, glaring at Kendra.

"Well, she should have signed the papers," Kendra said. Noticing the unpleasant looks on Satin and Zandra's faces, Kendra retreated to the door. "I think I'll go look for Keisha."

"Don't let her get to you."

"Kendra always speaks her mind," Satin said, shrugging. "And she's so suspicious and paranoid. I was in the wrong place at the wrong time. The police haven't said otherwise."

"For a while they were suspicious," Zandra said. "But the police have never come up with anything concrete." Satin paused thoughtfully. "I kind of hope they don't."

"If it was intentional—if you were shot because of the will and the shopping center—wouldn't you want to know?"

Satin shook her head.

"You don't want revenge? You don't want them to go to jail?"

"The police don't know anything. I'm not going to spend my life waiting for them to find out," Satin said. "If I worried about that, I probably wouldn't be—"

"Let's rewind back to happy thoughts," Zandra joyfully said. "Girl, you are stunning. Just stunning. Halle Berry ain't got nothing on you."

Satin laughed. "You sound like Aunt Maggie."

Zandra tapped her watch. "It's almost time."

Satin's heart dropped to the pit of her stomach. "I feel so nervous. This is a forever type of decision, and what if—"

"Are you going to marry him or are you going to be a runaway bride?"

"I'm not Julia Roberts." Her eyebrows drawn together, Satin had a look of contemplation. "Will we love each other forever and ever?"

"Satin, I was teasing before, but you do have a funny look on your face." Zandra shot her a piercing look. "You're not changing your mind, are you?"

"What if she changes her mind?" Drake asked Damon. "What if she stands me up?" They were inside the church sanctuary, standing near the altar. The church was crowded with family, relatives, and friends.

"She's not Tavia," Damon said, straightening the hanky in Drake's tuxedo pocket.

"I know. I know."

"She loves you, man. You know that."

"You're right." Drake looked at the back of the sanctuary, but saw no signs of the bride. It felt like déjà vu: the hush of excitement as everyone waited for the bride to appear. He dismissed the memory with the shake of his head. "Do you have the ring?"

Frowning, Damon patted the pockets of his tuxedo. He didn't feel the box. He then checked the inside pocket. "Of course I do," he said, smiling.

"Good."

"So what happened with the police?"

"They arrested a man for robbing a bank. The police found a gun in the bank robber's car that was traced to the gun that shot Satin."

"Did he shoot her?"

"He claims the gun wasn't his and he didn't do it."

"Right," Damon said sarcastically.

"He fingered somebody else and that person robbed the gas station. The police are trying to verify his story."

"Have you told Satin?"

"Not yet. I didn't want to cast a shadow over the wedding," Drake said. "The police don't know the full story yet. They're still investigating. When they know something definite, I think that'll be the time to tell her."

"She survived. That's all that matters."

"I don't believe he came," Drake said, waving at a middle-aged white couple.

"That's Walter Green. He's executive VP at Monet Cosmetics."

"They're still trying to get you to work for them?" Damon asked.

"Yeah. I'm happy where I am. The agency really took off after the 'If I Were Your Woman' campaign. I've had to almost double my staff."

Damon patted his brother on the back. "You the man, baby."

"It's fifteen minutes 'til." Drake's eyes rested on the clock on the back wall of church. "Satin hates being late."

Damon flicked his wrist to view his watch. "That clock's fast, man. She's coming."

At eight minutes until the hour, the bridal party began to move toward the front of the sanctuary. At two minutes 'til, the pianist played "The Wedding March" on the organ. Everyone in the church stood. At precisely two o'clock Satin entered the sanctuary, her hand tucked in her father's arm. Oliver escorted her down the aisle, past the whispered comments:

"Her gown is lovely."

"She is beautiful."

"She was having an affair with him."

"That's why she didn't marry that other boy."

"I heard he canceled the wedding."

"Look at the glow on her face. She's marrying the right one, now."

With each step Satin took toward the altar, Drake's heart rate accelerated in intensity and speed. Louder, faster, stronger, faster. By the time she reached him, Drake wondered if everyone in church could hear his heart.

"For a minute, I was worried you were going to run away," Drake whispered.

"How can I run from the rhythm of my heart?"

"You are my heart," Drake said, gazing deep into her eyes, a blissful smile on her face. "The reflection of my smile."

Dear Reader:

You've heard it—the little inner voice . . . intuition . . . God's voice. But sometimes we ignore it. Satin didn't just hear her inner voice, she heeded it. Her life-changing decision shocked her family and friends. But she chose a path of growth and self-discovery.

Did Satin make the right decision to leave her fiancée and move to Atlanta? Had she stayed, she wouldn't have met Drake Swanson. Wasn't his mother a trip? Should Satin have sold her inheritance? Do you know a woman like Aunt Maddie who's never recovered from a love affair?

Please share with me your reactions and opinions. You can e-mail me at ROB2ALLEN@aol.com. Or send a letter to P.O. Box 673634, Marietta, GA 30006. Be sure to enclose a self-addressed, stamped envelope for a faster response.

I appreciate your E-mails and letter about THE PROMISE. My next book will be about Romare's little sister, Tangi Ellington.

Love and happiness,
Robin Allen

ABOUT THE AUTHOR

Robin Hampton Allen is the author of **The Promise, Hidden Memories** and **Breeze.** Her feature articles have been published in national publications, including *Black Elegance, Belle, Today's Black Woman* and *Diversity Careers.* In 2001, Ms. Allen was included in Women Looking Ahead Newsmagazine 100s List of Georgia's Most Powerful & Influential Women—Arts & Entertainment. Ms. Allen has extensive experience in marketing communications and public relations in the high-tech industry.

Ms. Allen grew up in Pittsburgh, Pennsylvania and graduated from the University of Pittsburgh. She lives in Atlanta, Georgia with her two daughters. She enjoys reading, traveling, and attending plays and movies. She is working on her next novel.

More Sizzling Romance From
Brenda Jackson

__One Special Moment	0-7860-0546-7	**$4.99**US/**$6.50**CAN
__Tonight and Forever	0-7860-0172-0	**$4.99**US/**$5.99**CAN
__Whispered Promises	1-58314-097-2	**$5.99**US/**$7.99**CAN
__Eternally Yours	0-7860-0455-X	**$4.99**US/**$6.50**CAN
__Secret Love	1-58314-073-5	**$5.99**US/**$7.99**CAN
__Fire and Desire	1-58314-024-7	**$4.99**US/**$6.50**CAN
__True Love	1-58314-144-8	**$5.99**US/**$7.99**CAN

More Sizzling Romances From *Carmen Green*

__Now or Never	0-7860-0327-8	**$4.99**US/**$6.50**CAN
__Keeping Secrets	0-7860-0494-0	**$4.99**US/**$6.50**CAN
__Silken Love	1-58314-095-6	**$5.99**US/**$7.99**CAN
__Endless Love	1-58314-135-9	**$5.99**US/**$7.99**CAN
__Commitments	1-58314-226-6	**$5.99**US/**$7.99**CAN